MW00479158

Trip Mackintosh has loved the people of Africa since he served as a US Peace Corps Volunteer (Morocco 1979-81). He became an internationally recognized lawyer in the areas of trade controls and white-collar crime. Much of his work involved matters in Africa. During the last forty years, he has traveled and lived in fourteen African countries. In creating his characters and settings, he draws on his substantial experience in the African bush and with its people. This has included training as a safari guide in the Okavango Delta and one-on-one mentoring by a

Bushman elder in the Kalahari Desert. With this unique background, he is able to take readers from glass-walled conference rooms in New York skyscrapers to the shifting sands of the Kalahari. His writing presents a rich view of Africa and a compelling glimpse into its troubled history. He does this with compassion and demonstrable respect for the complexity of African people and cultures. He is married with four children, two of whom were adopted from Zambia. His next work of fiction will center on the female anti-poaching squad of Zambia and their incredible bravery.

Rebuild the Moon

Cover photographs by the author.

Trip Mackintosh

Rebuild the Moon

Vanguard Press

VANGUARD PAPERBACK

© Copyright 2023

Trip Mackintosh

The right of Trip Mackintosh to be identified as author of
this work has been asserted by them in accordance with the
Copyright, Designs and Patents Act 1988.

A CIP catalogue record for this title is
available from the British Library.

ISBN 978 1 80016 929 6

*Vanguard Press is an imprint of
Pegasus Elliot Mackenzie Publishers Ltd.*
www.pegasuspublishers.com

First Published in 2023

**Vanguard Press
Sheraton House Castle Park
Cambridge England**

Printed & Bound in Great Britain

For Qxatta

My thanks to Mark Rollinger for his friendship and steady editor's pen, to Gareth Peake for introducing me to the African bush, and to my partner in life and writing, Whitney.

Contents

Preface

Inspiration for this novel came when driving alone to meet with an elder Bushman, Qxatta. He had agreed to take me into the Kalahari. I was to be his student; he, my tutor. When I met him late one evening at a lodge in Botswana, he presented himself with such simple dignity — his small frame, leather briefs, walking stick and smile were about all he had. Yet through his eyes and the relationship we subsequently developed, he shared with me the wealth of his Kalahari home.

Patiently pulling open a curtain, he showed me the Kodachrome colors with which he saw the desert — tracks of eland became brilliant crisscrossing cuts of distinct hooves in the sand; drab bushes, seemingly the same, each radiated with uniqueness, and the sand itself turned into a book. Most importantly, he opened himself to me, showing how the desert was part of who he was while displaying significant grace, humility, and a watershed of spontaneous humor.

Rebuild the Moon is a fictionalized account based on actual histories of indiscriminate violence and persecution San people suffered well into the 1950s. The story is my modest tribute to the San people, their singular way of life, courage, and tremendous resilience.

"If you offend, ask for pardon;
If offended, forgive."

African Proverb

Part I

Confession and Conflict

Chapter 1

Dagga Boy

His rifle rocked slightly a few degrees up and down with each tilt showing the way down a trail squeezed between mopane and buffalo thorn. He paused, both boots still in deep dust, his weapon motionless, horizontal. Air whispered warmly down the path, toward his face, bringing smells of the bush. Sniffing, he raised his nose.

Sometimes, you can smell them.

Flies found him with the breeze. They troubled his eyes, explored his face, and walked around his closed lips. He blinked them away without moving his head. A bird pushed through dried leaves to his left. He did not move, only listened.

After a hundred safaris, oil from his hands darkened the stock and grip of his .375 H&H Magnum. The rifle now carried part of him. His habit of allowing the weapon to pivot in his left hand as he walked had changed his gait. He now needed the gun to feel balanced when on a hunt. The rifle's weight and motion also provided necessary reassurance. He was a short, slight man in the

African bush where a hundred things can crush, gore, and kill.

He signaled, pointing down behind his back. In the middle of the trail was a mound of green dung, still wet, steaming. He stepped over it slowly.

Msizi, his hunting partner, saw the gesture. A Zulu, he was a good head taller than Jon. He followed several paces back. As black is to white, Msizi's presence on the trail was different from Jon's. Graceful in the bush, Msizi had grown up barefoot, chasing his family's cattle near the uMzinyathi River in the east of South Africa.

The Zulu walked easily, his rifle seemingly weightless in his left hand, his shoulders level. The tight trail, the buffalo somewhere in front of them — it was all part of him. He was smooth, attentive, without effort. This was his place.

Jon looked back at Msizi, telegraphing with his expression.

This old man's close. We've got him.

Msizi smiled. Shifting his eyes from Jon to the bush on either side, holding his rifle solidly in a large hand, he motioned forward with his chin at the trail in front of them.

I should be leading. Don't look back at me, Jon. You worry me when you do. Keep your eyes where they should be. You don't need to show me what I can see. These dry mopane leaves, they're too quiet. Something's coming.

His back to Msizi, Jon knelt and placed fingers on kidney-shaped halves of buffalo prints.

Not deep. Flat, regular.

They were almost as large as his hand. His firearm remained level as he moved up the trail, squatted, and traced the outline of another print.

He's kicking dirt in front of his prints, not behind. This old man is just walking. He doesn't know we're here. two thousand pounds of black death taking a stroll.

"Black death" fit the beast. More than any other animal, a solitary Cape Buffalo bull embodies the danger and unpredictability of the African bush. Pushed by younger males out of the herd, he stands alone against predation. He has but two ears, two eyes and one muzzle to pick up scents, movement, and danger. A herd has hundreds of each. A solo buffalo compensates by being reflexive, relying on almost a ton of explosive force, crushing hooves and an impenetrable head of horns to forestall the inevitable: death by lion.

Like all lone bulls, the buffalo they tracked was this dark mix of fury and strength. Spark him with a scent or a crack of a stick — and prey becomes predator. It will be a straight on rush, head down, enormous horns sweeping right and left. When hooking his prey and launching it into the air with an easy twist of his massive neck, the solitary bull will have a look of disdain, almost boredom. Such bloody violence is the life of a dagga boy.

For years Jon had wanted a trophy bull. His fingers tracing the tracks, he thought of when, still a boy, he and his father were lunching in a Cape Town pub. Next to them were two drunk Boer farmers, loudly recounting lies about hunting — leaning on the bar, with big, scarred forearms lifting pints.

Seeing Jon next to them, one turned, gently put his calloused hand on Jon's back, spanning most of it. "Small as you are, seun, what do you hunt? Duiker maybe?"

"Yes, sir, I have. But they don't have much meat. What do you hunt?"

"I'll put a duiker or two in my pocket for breakfast when going out. My favorite? Dagga boys. They'll show you a good time."

Jon remembered the man's face, swollen from sun and beer, blue eyes deep set.

"Sorry, sir, dagga boys?"

"Solo bulls. The meanest thing out there. Lions will run from you. Rhinos will go right past you if you hold still. You can talk with olifants. They listen.

"Dagga boys are black monsters. They will hunt you, ambush you, and open you up. We call them dagga boys because they wear wallow mud, dagga, making them look crazier than they are."

The image of a black monster and the weight of the farmer's massive hand left a deep impression on Jon. When the Boer turned back to his beer and companion, he left the boy with images of a deadly beast in the bush, and a goal: when he could, he would go for a dagga boy.

Jon began hunting when only five-years-old. His family had a hilly farm in the Western Cape. He and his father would hunt in the early morning or late afternoon.

He told Jon, "No sense going out if the beasts are asleep under a bush. When they start hunting, we will."

Under his father's care, each hunt was a teaching session mixed with adventure and adrenaline.

He had a clear memory of one of his first. It was cold with the sun just rising over the mountains. His father preferred the morning to late afternoon. "The light's better." Fog of his breath clouded his view of his father a few feet in front. Still small, he carried a bird gun that was not loaded.

Annoyed by the weight of the gun, the cold, and lack of action, Jon whined, "Dad, can't we find something quickly and go home? It's freezing and I'm hungry."

His father stopped, turned, and knelt at Jon's eye level.

He put his hand on the boy's shoulder. "Son, no matter if it is hot or cold, if you are after an impala or a leopard, you have to take with you on every hunt two things: routine and patience. You need routine so that if your brain is not working well enough at the moment, your body knows what to do. You need patience to give your brain time to do what it needs to do. If you don't have both with you on every hunt, you'll lose. If you become restless or impulsive because you lost your patience, or you or your weapon isn't ready because you did not follow your routine, the bush may kill you. Can you promise me you'll remember?"

Jon smiled a 'yes,' as his father gently shoved his shoulder.

Instilling these essentials, his father coached Jon over the years. He would test Jon on one element and then the other. Jon had to prepare his rifle and test his rounds just before every hunt, not the day before, only as they were leaving for the bush. Even if Jon had performed the same exercise the day before with the same bullets, his father would watch to ensure that Jon chambered each round — once again — to confirm its proper fit. That was routine. As for patience, often he would stop the boy with a hand signal, motioning his son to hold still. He tested the child's limits, often having him stand motionless for fifteen minutes or more for no apparent reason.

One lesson on the combined value of routine and patience was so sharp that it carved a permanent place for itself in Jon's childhood nightmares. He was nine, walking behind his father east of their farm where forested hills started a slow rise to the Cederberg Mountains. It was a year before his father would disappear for the war in Europe.

The goal was an impala, one of many nearby. But many and nearby meant little with impala, Jon knew. Taking an impala could be like clutching at quicksilver, with lithe antelope flowing out of grasp at the slightest disruption.

Jon now hunted with a loaded rifle, a short magazine Lee-Enfield Mk III. His father had packed the .303 rounds himself. He had handloaded them with less powder so Jon could withstand the rifle's kick. These weaker rounds shortened the gun's effectiveness, and that suited his father's designs. The goal was to teach Jon the essentials of bush hunting. "A long-distance shot," he said, "is more about bragging rights than hunting."

The afternoon sun at their backs cast long shadows in front of them as they left a stand of trees. Before them, with colors enhanced by the sunlight, a dozen impala fed, heads down, tails flicking in a field that seemed artificially bright green. A guardian buck raised his head from time to time. He seemed to look straight at them, causing Jon and his father to freeze, and then returned to grazing. A light wind blew from the antelope to the man and boy. If Jon and his father were quiet and careful, with wind in their face, sun at their back, and the shadows of the trees behind them, they could approach undetected. About fifty meters from the herd, his father motioned to him to lie flat and rest his barrel on a dirt mound.

"Son, relax," he whispered. "Be gentle with your rifle. Your body, your muscles, they know how to shoot. Let them do their work. Rely on your routine. Don't let your thoughts get in the way."

Hand lightly on Jon's back, he added softly, "Remember, another part of our routine is: we never lose sight of where we are. Keep an eye open all around. We might not be the only hunters here."

Jon exhaled halfway, held his breath, and sighted on a doe who had lifted her head. He squeezed off a round aiming for her shoulder. He missed. The herd bolted, like a rush of brown, black, and white water pouring quickly in waves out of sight. At the same instant, a leopard broke cover within meters of them. It fled silently into the bush back toward the trees. Jon watched it run, taking with it his self-confidence.

Growing up in that area of Africa, he knew the perils of large cats. Leopards were the most dangerous, stalking at night near farms. Children were just the right size to be taken and dragged into the night.

He began to cry, shoulders slouched. "Sorry, Papa. I should've known he was there."

His father knelt, facing Jon, wiping a tear from the boy's cheek, then putting both hands reassuringly on his shoulders.

"Son, routine is more than lining up a good shot. You can plan perfectly. You can be the best tracker, with the best back up. You can know the terrain. The sun, shadows, and wind can favor you. But the beast you're hunting, or another, might have its own ideas for you.

"If you plan only for what you expect, that plan may kill you. You've got to keep yourself, your weapon, and your expectations loose, flexible. Rely on a solid habit of listening, waiting, and studying the bush around you and the soil under your boots. Use your patience to adjust your approach based on what you detect.

"Remember," gesturing around them, "this bush is a minefield. Explosives with claws and teeth are everywhere.

"You focused only on your target. Those baboons high above were warning us, talking to you, Jon. If you had listened to them, they would have told you a predator was here. If you had glanced down, you would have seen cat's prints winding to where we were going. His spoor was fresh, the earth still wet in his prints, and they were large, a big male. I heard the alarm calls and knew they were for something. I predicted where he was. He was using the sun, dark trees, and the wind — just like we were. Next time, you'll see him too."

He stood and rested a hand on Jon's shoulder, jostling it softly.

"Make sure your chamber is empty and the pin engaged. Keep it safe, boy. Let's go home and tell mother about the impala you almost had."

By his twenties, Jon was a refined product of his father's training. Every morning before a hunt, he would inspect his rifle, slowly verifying everything was clean and working, double-checking sights. He would test the spring in the magazine. He would take each round, chamber it, check for fit, even if the same bullet had been spun the day before. It was a matter of doing things right, following routine, where there is no margin for error.

His unyielding routine tested the patience of hunting partners, who, driven by adrenaline or over-confidence, wanted to get to it quickly. He would not go out with them unless they, too, performed the same gun and ammunition ritual, not the night before, but always the morning of the hunt.

He shot frequently to keep his body trained to respond reflexively, correctly, knowing that he might not have time to think. He timed himself, to maintain his ability to insert a round, aim and shoot accurately within half a second. Even that, he knew, might be too slow.

On the spoor of this shuffling, slow-moving dagga boy, Jon had the sun at his back and the wind in his face, as he had that day years before. Imitating his father, he squatted at a green mound of fresh wet dung, almost smelling it, feeling its heat, inspecting left and right, low, under the branches. He saw nothing there, no dark legs of their bull, no flicking tails of a predator. He breathed deeply while standing, placing his footfalls lightly on the tan sand, his eyes scanning left, right, up, down, with his peripheral vision finding openings between thin, dark trunks and branches and the dead leaves they held.

To his left, he heard a crack. He folded down, knees flexed, on the ready. Msizi did the same. Both sought a bush or tree trunk that might actually be a leg or movement that would signal buffalo or a lion, unseen, meters away.

A sweet thorn bush on his right snagged his shirt. He pulled and tore a hole in the sleeve, adding to a punctured forearm. His left was fine. He had kept that arm balanced protectively against his side, gently cradling his .375.

Another branch snap and then quickly another sounded to his right. Jon shifted, sweeping his rifle across his chest, chambering a round, stock put to his right shoulder, as he had done a thousand times. Simultaneously, he stepped forward with his left foot, knees slightly bent, to prepare his shot.

As if he had stepped off a ledge into air, his boot found no purchase, nothing. His body followed his left leg down into a maw of empty, into red African earth that widened to swallow him. Frantic, he threw his rifle and clawed, straining for black hands he saw that were reaching for him. He grabbed them as they gripped his wrists. They pulled him back, held him firmly, keeping him from falling further.

His eyes widened, darting with fear, then relaxed in recognition. It was not Msizi. He had died long ago. Patrick, his nurse, looked at him with practiced compassion, moving a pillow under Jon's head. Jon reached up and touched the man's face.

"Thank you, Patrick."

Patrick smiled. "You were dreaming of the hunt again? Did you shoot the lion, Mr. Schmidt?"

While he spoke, he moved to the other side of the bed. "Let me get that IV back in. You made a mess."

Jon relaxed, looking out the window as Patrick reinserted the needle. Turning back, he could see blood on the sheets.

"There was blood that day too. A lot of it. That old bull came on us so fast."

"So, no lion this time, a bull?"

"Not a lion, son. Not that day. But could have been a lion, easily, in that worthless scrub southeast of Hoedspruit. More lions there than tsetse flies. Both can kill you, but I would rather go by lion. Fast, you know. They crush their prey's throat. It's usually over quickly. Going by sleeping sickness is, well, rather like how I am dying now, in pieces, bits of me sloughing off, taking forever."

Patrick raised his eyes at Jon as he worked to get the stained sheets off the bed.

No doubt, dying here is slow, Mr. Schmidt. Not sure a lion is a better option.

Mr. Jon Schmidt, formerly of South Africa, was dissipating slowly, dying between high-count cotton sheets in a high-end New York hospice. St. Lawrence, of Manhattan, was for the wealthy, for those with money enough to have their lives end slowly, with careful, costly ministrations. Lions would have been a better choice for many than the bit-by-bit erosion that seemed to take forever in St. Lawrence.

Patrick had been with Jon since his cancer brought him to this Varanasi-on-the-Hudson several months earlier. Smoothing out the fresh bed linens, Patrick smiled at Jon. He was one of so many Patrick had lifted lightly over life's transom. Jon was different, though. His mind, his passion, was not with his money and the inevitable loss of it. Jon, he found, was elsewhere.

When he arrived at St Lawrence, Jon's cancer was well established, moving into organs, and pushing out of grasp any more years of life. To Patrick, it seemed that Jon accepted the cancer and the end it was bringing but was troubled by something else — something unsettled, unfair.

On the day of his admission, he had waved his thin white arms around his room of sunlit, large windows, preaching to Patrick, "Death, itself, doesn't care about any of this. I have seen it come to a hut, on a trail in the bush, as comfortably as it will come here.

"My family — well, most of my family — thinks all of this matters. For them, the luxurious, expensive care of this place will mean an elegant passing; the elegance they arrange will compensate for the large estate I leave behind. Ultimately, you know, your life just goes. The money, the place, doesn't matter." He fell silent, brooding. "What matters are unpaid debts."

Patrick had leaned in that day, placing a hand on Jon's shoulder, "Mr. Schmidt, we all go out the same door, money trailing us or not, debts unpaid or not. I've seen many men standing on the moment of passing over. On that edge, between life and death, I've seen wealthy men struggle and poor men relax. I think it's more what's in your head, that's what makes it easy or hard."

Jon sighed, his small chest compressing, "What's in my head we need to talk about. The rest of it, not so sure. No sense moaning over an eighty-five-year-old alcoholic chain smoker dying of cancer. Seems to me the recipe worked. Radiation and chemo dropping into the batter, not adding much, now, is it?"

He pinched his own arm, then turned over his flat hands. "Look at that, you can almost see through me. What's there to radiate? Machine might miss me altogether." He chuckled.

"Now for my head," he told Patrick, more darkly. "My Africa is gone. I lost it years ago. My friends as well. My largest debt remains unpaid. The only part of me doing full bore are my investments. As my financial wealth increases, so does this debt."

That conversation had been only a few months ago. Jon had markedly, quickly, deteriorated. Now, after waking from his nightmare of the dagga boy hunt, the dying man looked again at his hands, turning them over. *A scarecrow's hands, desiccated, blue veins reflecting a dying anatomy. They failed. They're a map of failures.*

He pushed against the pillow. A cannula weakly wheezed oxygen into his nose. He held his left hand against his face, pressing the fitting closer, taking a deep breath.

"Patrick, would you call my lawyer, Ms. Epstein? She's, I think, number one in my list of favorites. Need to talk about the estate."

He laughed a bit, finding the young man in himself. She was first in his contacts because she was gorgeous. Partner at the firm that had shepherded his fortune from South Africa to the US, she specialized in wills of high-net-worth clients.

With money came conflict. Ms. Epstein, Georgetown Law, was an elegant gladiator. She was lithe, poised, and polished. In his fantasies, he imagined her manicured claws could retract.

When they had first met, he had instantly found her compelling — the way her body and hands moved with confidence, the way her green eyes met his.

Smiling at her, he had thought, she's graceful, beautiful, ready when her territory is violated, a boundary is crossed or if she feels like it. Like a leopard, deceptively calm, silent, and stunning until then.

He closed his eyes, readying for her arrival with thoughts of himself as a younger man.

Chapter 2

Big Cats

It was mid-afternoon when Julia Epstein's soft knock, faint steps, scent, and an intimate, "Hello, Jon," announced her.

She entered with an enthusiasm he imagined was only for him. He smiled and moved his shoulders back.

She's back in my territory.

When she bent to kiss his cheek, he let himself travel into her perfume, feeling her hair on his face, for a moment letting himself go. He closed pink lids over pale blue eyes, white lashes touching top to bottom, otherwise holding himself still, anticipating her touch.

Pressing her hand lightly on his chest, she said, "Behave yourself, Jon. Meet my colleague, Justin. He's helping me with your file. Justin, Mr. Schmidt is my favorite client, a man of brilliant stories, some of which he says are true."

Jon shifted from Julia to the young lawyer, the other male now in his zone. He assessed him in seconds. No threat.

Young Justin, if you wanted to present yourself in a way that, without speaking, told me that you are earnest, and to be trusted, you've achieved it. Tight haircut, good suit, fine posture, young but tired already in the eyes, all tell me you are dedicated to who you are, which is your work. I bet you think everything matters.

You'll do just fine.

"Sit down, son, relax if that's possible. But first, reach into the closet. Get me a cigarette."

Justin caught himself in mid-sit, turned toward the closet, then hesitated, glancing at the oxygen tube on Jon's face.

Patrick intervened, "Mr. Schmidt, don't torture the boy."

"OK, Justin. Just take a chair. Tell me what you've written up so far."

Julia walked to a window, Jon tracked her with his eyes, his head unmoving, watching her legs move, listening to her soft footfalls. His nostrils discretely flared to follow her scent.

Justin began reading from his laptop.

"Mr. Jon Schmidt, you, sir, apologies for the use of the third person, immigrated from South Africa to the US in 1956."

Jon smiled with his eyes closed, "Go on, boy, don't worry about formalities, get to it."

"Thank you, sir. Several years later, Mr. Schmidt's father passed away in Cape Town, leaving his businesses to his only child, you, sir. The South African holdings were diversified. Mr. Schmidt's grandfather had founded a trucking firm with the advent of petroleum engines in the early 1900s. He succeeded by developing a network of supply and grocery depots throughout the country. From those, small trucks would deliver supplies to individual farms and isolated towns. Over time, the depots became stores and the isolated towns, larger towns. Roads were improved. The result was a food and goods distribution network that grew from modest roots in the Cape to a trucking and supermarket chain across South Africa. The integration of trucking and retail gave the company flexibility during periods of fluctuation in the prices of petrol or food stock. This allowed the Schmidt Companies to survive when others failed.

"The wars, to include regional and global conflicts, such as the World Wars, led to further diversification. Schmidt Companies won key supply contracts for South African armed forces. The British government selected these companies to meet logistic and supply requirements in the Southern Atlantic during and after World War II. This added oceanic shipping to a growing family of companies.

"Mr. Jon Schmidt, our client, inherited controlling interests in this shipping and grocery empire in the late 1950s. Increasingly uncomfortable with South African government racial policies in the 1960s and early 1970s, Mr. Schmidt began a series of divestitures that resulted in his fortune coming to the United States.

"At present, he holds approximately $100 million in liquid assets, including securities and bonds. Another $20 million is invested in real estate. His homes in New York City and Martha's Vineyard are part of this portion of his portfolio."

Justin cleared his throat, putting his small fist up against his mouth. He looked up at Jon. Julia, still at the window, was motionless, but for half-squinted eyes that moved with the people on the street. Jon's attention was on her, not Justin.

Not looking away from Julia, he said, "Boy, you ever hunt?"

"Excuse me, sir?"

"Have you ever hunted?" Jon repeated while trying to sit up.

Justin started into "No, but I wish I had" in a way that he thought would please his firm's client — when suddenly, Jon groaned and grabbed his nearly hairless head with both thin hands.

"Damn, Patrick. The pain is back. I can't think or hear this boy."

"Yessir. Remember to press the lever. You control the pain. Use the lever. Stay ahead of the pain."

Jon gave the morphine dispenser a few squeezes.

"Right. Sorry. Don't want to become a junkie, you know. Been there once. Bad enough I am dying of cancer. Can't have my reputation ruined again on the way out.

"OK, son, keep going with the legal stuff. But, before you do, I must know who I'm working with. Have you ever hunted?"

The only thing Justin had hunted was admission to Yale Law School and an elite law firm job.

"No, sir. Wish I had," he repeated, adding, "I understand you did."

Julia smiled at Justin's courtesies as she moved to a chair. For his part, Jon, the hunter, assessed Julia through her well-fitted suit. He straightened, sitting taller, nostrils rapidly opening and closing, finding her. He felt the air around her move.

Turning back to the young lawyer, he said, "Listen, Justin, I hunted, too much maybe. Conceit, you know. Was all about being a grand hunter. Some hunts were good, some tragic. We'll talk later about those. For now, let's get back to your report."

Justin continued, "Shortly after arrival in the United States, Mr. Schmidt married. He divorced some twenty years later, and that matter is settled. He has two adult children and three grandchildren.

"With the assistance of our firm, Cogswell & Worthy, Mr. Schmidt established a revocable trust to pay for the education of the grandchildren and to assist them after university. Currently, the trust manages tuition and other costs and has provisions to assist with homes and business investments as the grandchildren age.

"Mr. Schmidt's last will and testament provides that 90% of liquid assets shall be divided equally between his two children through a series of trusts and other structures designed to reduce or eliminate estate tax liabilities. The balance of the liquid assets will go to several charities in South Africa.

"Real estate assets will be maintained by a separate trust for the use and enjoyment of his children, grandchildren and great-grandchildren consistent with New York law. Per requirements of applicable law, any assets exceeding a lawful period of inheritance will be liquidated and remanded to the estate to be divided per the trusts and other structures previously mentioned, to secure their proper disposition in accordance with the wishes of Mr. Schmidt."

Jon was snoring. The legal language and morphine had had their effect.

Eyes closed, mouth open, he did not react when Julia approached the bed and leaned in.

"Jon, should we leave to give you some rest?"

Patrick moved to the bedside. "There is a chance he will be under for a few hours. I can let you know."

Picking up her bag, Julia glanced at the screen of her phone, lit green with messages. Scrolling through them as she walked to the door, she handed Patrick a card.

"Justin and I will get dinner nearby. Jon wanted to meet with us today. We'll stay available and close."

Justin stepped back to allow her to leave the room first, shortening his stride so as not to crowd her. He turned his head and caught Jon's face moving. The old man was talking with someone.

Jon was back home in the Cape of his youth, a teenager, hunting with his father. His dad had left for the war in Europe four years before and had returned different, distant, slower. Jon was trying to read him, to understand who he had become.

Jon was a few paces behind when his father's boots scraped abruptly to a stop. Jon all but bumped him. He mimicked his father, holding still, not knowing why. Peering around, he saw, meters in front of them, a young male lion. Hidden by a coat the color of the bush, body prone, all but invisible on the dirt and among dried grasses, the cat stared at them. He panted; eyes locked on Jon's father. All three were motionless, but for the animal's breathing and a black-tipped tail that, to Jon, seemed to be spastically ticking off the seconds before the probable attack.

Jon kept his weapon down, watching his father, looking up at the back of his shoulders, seeing them rise and then relax, nothing, nothing. His father's rifle was not lifting. It remained angled to the dirt, his wrist drooping with calm, as though he was standing there for no reason.

Papa! Why is your rifle down? Chamber a round, you might have time. I can't without noise that might make him charge; you must. I can't get a shot with you in front of me. What are you doing?

Jon's father, apparently uncaring, his thin frame preternaturally loose, relaxed in front of this killer. His arms hung limp, useless.

The war had physically diminished his father, as it had emptied his spirit. He was disconnected from home, from Jon, from his wife, even though he was physically there, among them.

That morning, his wife had seen how distracted he was.

"Don't go out today. Stay home with me, Carl. Just close your eyes. You've been staring at nothing for minutes now. I worry about you out there. You need rest, to recover."

"No, I'm quite all right. Just need some bush time with my boy, I'll be fine."

That afternoon, his father had started their hunt, as he seemed to begin every one of them since his return, by telling Jon, "I know it's been hard since I got back. I lost my footing over there. I think, this is how I can get home, really. I can find my old self out here. Let's go. You're a good tracker. Help me find it."

Almost six feet tall, Carl was down to barely one hundred and sixty pounds after his military service. His old hunting boots, Jon noticed, now looked cartoonishly large. His clothes sagged. His thin wrists fell out of seemingly oversized sleeves.

Leaving their truck on the edge of the farm, they had wound up, single file, through cedars and bush that softened rocky hills leading to the Cederberg Mountains.

Sharp, low cliffs north of them rose precipitously from thick brush. They hunted against these cliffs, son behind father, studying soil crisscrossed with tracks of kudu, impala, and eland. In their silent focus, walking slowly, studying the movement of wildlife recorded in the sand, man and boy found quiet where the man could think.

Several hours from the truck, Jon's father had paused at some spoor, clear, fresh hoof imprints cut into sandy soil between rocks. He quizzed his son:

"What is it?"

Bent on a knee, tracing the prints with his fingers, Jon replied, "Eland, Papa, maybe a small giraffe?"

His father shook his head, "Too long for eland. I say, young giraffe. Now, bull or cow?"

Jon's eyes scrutinized the tracks.

How do I tell gender from tracks like these? It's a young giraffe.

"Remember, not all answers are in the prints, son." Motioning back to a game trail that ran against the rocks, he added, "It's on this track, but not here. Think, Jon."

Seemingly tired from giving this modest instruction, his father turned his neck upward, mouth open in a yawn. It appeared to Jon that he wanted to swallow the air around him. The man shifted his weight to his good leg and settled watching the trail in front of them, his back to his boy.

Jon glanced at his father while turning to walk the faint trace of a game trail, backward and then forward. He looked at the bushes for signs of browsing. He read the dirt at his feet. There, the answer was ten meters back: droppings, giraffe dung.

Jon picked up a pellet. It was fresh from that afternoon. It was concave on both ends.

"Female."

"Good lad, let's move. A young cow alone just might invite a lion or two. Replace your first two rounds with soft points."

Making the switch with bullets from his belt, Jon thought, *With any luck, we'll get a cat, not a giraffe.*

The giraffe's tracks turned west at the base of two large, oblong boulders. Following them into the afternoon sun — where the hunters would be exposed — was a risk with lions likely about, but the cover seemed fine. The wind was good, blowing toward them.

This is what I missed, Papa. You and me, here, on edge, alive, danger and risk just part of the day, together. So missed you.

His father had served the Crown in Germany, fighting an army of predators unleashed by Hitler. He came home with thrilling after-dinner stories and a dragging limp. All that was required to kick off some stories were his pipe and scotch. The limp got in the way. It required painkillers on bad days and patience when on a hunt.

The leg injury, his father said, was "nothing."

"I was clumsy getting out of a lorry."

I don't believe you, Papa. More like taking a round in the thigh while hunting a German division by yourself.

In the rocks that afternoon, while on the young giraffe cow's track, Jon had been focused on his father's slow limp and the prints it made. A dangerous thing to do when hunting, he let his mind wander, imagining what his father had done in Europe and thinking that a wounded man might well be seen as prey out in the bush. He was in those thoughts when his father unexpectedly halted in front of the lion.

Carefully, noiselessly, Jon now looked around his father's legs.

He touched him on the back. *Move. I'll take the shot. Move aside.*

His father stayed still. A light wind in their faces smelled of blood.

Jon's grip tightened on his rifle.

He inhaled through his nose, trying to pick up the scent of lion or anything else. A deep, quick breath and Jon coughed, then panicked thinking the noise would spark a charge.

He tried to sit up. Patrick stood up from his chair.

"Nice nap?"

"Sorry. What? Was back in the Cape. It was the day I shot my first lion, also the day my dad seemed to want to die. Told you about it."

"

I want to hear it again. Maybe later? Should I call back the lawyers?"

"Yes, call them. Let's get to this."

Chapter 3

Burden Shift

"Thanks for the break," Jon said, trying to sit up for Julia, pushing his shoulders back and his thin chest out. His eyes did not leave hers as she moved toward his bed.

"Did you get some rest?" softly touching only hairs on his forearm.

He looked at her hand, hovering just above, but still touching his skin. She let it rest a moment too long, moved it gently back and forth and lifted it slowly. He followed it to her shoulder and then continued to her face.

"I know I've told you about my first lion. That's where I was thanks to this high-quality opium, they're pumping into me."

Looking from Julia to Justin, he said, "I wanted you today to discuss the estate. Figured it out. As we say at home, 'dit is klaar.'" His voice and eyes, too, were clear as he turned to address the young legal draftsman.

"Changing my will. Completely."

Julia twitched. Regardless of the motive or the revisions, there would be a fight. There was so much money at stake. She loved a fight. And a fight meant fees. She curled her fingers into the palms of both hands.

To keep her nails retracted, Jon noticed, smiling to himself.

Justin opened his laptop to take down word-for-word what Mr. Schmidt said. Patrick tilted back in his chair on two legs, resting it against the wall.

Rich white people can be so dramatic. This'll be good.

Jon spoke in an even, matter-of-fact voice, slowed by the drugs, but strong. "All of my liquid assets will go to a new trust, established in South Africa or Namibia, whatever you figure out is best. My real estate will remain for the benefit of my heirs here.

"The new trust will benefit through education, health and other development the heirs and clan members of the Bushmen I hunted in 1955."

Julia cut in, "Bushmen you hunted *with*," she corrected. "Got it."

Jon only turned his light blue eyes to her, gravely, intently, silently narrowing them.

She turned to Patrick. "Could you give us a few minutes?"

"No," Jon said. "Patrick, please stay."

For the first time since Julia had entered the room, Jon looked away from her. He seemed to fix on a point on the wall behind her. He sighed heavily.

"The funds from the new trust will be used to establish schools, a small hospital, hire teachers, doctors, and administrators, set up a cultural center and provide for higher education for those who want it. I want the center to specialize in San Bushman languages and art."

He waited. She did not respond. He was going to have to make the clarification explicit.

"The Bushmen I hunted," he repeated. "The two Bushmen I hunted.'"

His listeners were going to need a moment to absorb this. The only sound was the faint hiss from Jon's oxygen and the muffled growl of Manhattan traffic.

"We hunted them, tracked them for days. The guy I was with shot one. I could've stopped him. Didn't. I was a coward. Other Bushmen died because I lied about what happened. So, there it is. My confession, why I'm changing my will."

It had come out quickly. No one spoke. Jon looked at them one by one.

He broke the silence, "Justin, make a note, they are called San or San Bushmen. Be sure you get it right."

"Yes, sir."

"Julia, it's not the drugs or disease talking. I've never been clearer on what I want.

"It was a different time, a bad time. It was brutal.

"I was a drunk, foolish. I got swept up in racist propaganda about Black Africans.

"This guy, this murderer, talked me into going. He convinced me to pay for this grand volunteer expedition to protect white farmers. It was bullshit.

"He was a manipulating, calculating human-hunter. Plain and simple. I was a dupe. I was the guy who shelled out for everything, even his bullets. Didn't have the courage to stop it. Could've."

He coughed loudly.

Eyes watering, face red, he said, "You got enough? You can see I'm dying. Need to fix this *now*."

Julia lowered her head and turned to Justin, signaling the importance of the conversation and the need for his notes to be accurate.

"Jon, another minute if you can. I'm not sure I understand the context of all this. You were some sort of militia? You were with some other man?"

"Yeah, that's it, that's the best spin on it. Militia." He waved his hand to dismiss her attempt at advocacy. It was time for truth. "More like vigilantes. Back then, white farmers across Africa feared attack. Mau Mau and their victims in Kenya were in the press every day.

"This monster and I, we went into South West Africa, me thinking that I was some sort of volunteer going to help out. Learned too late that he just was going for the — the *sport*."

The word sat there incongruously in the middle of the room where Jon had placed it. Outside on the streets of Manhattan, there was the usual muted honking of car horns.

"The sport of hunting and killing Bushmen."

Jon laughed and choked at the same time. Patrick, eyebrows raised in disbelief, moved in to wipe his mouth and respectfully returned to his chair.

After catching his breath, Jon continued, "He was a murderer and a fool. Going after a San Bushman on foot can be deadly. Was for him. Like following a mamba in the sand. You might do it, finding its whip tracks, you see? But the end might not be what you had in mind. It'll kill you.

"Bushmen are the best hunters in Africa. They're tough, resilient. As I said, he had shot one. That poor boy didn't die right away. He and his partner somehow managed to kill this murderer before the wounded Bushman died. The survivor could've killed me."

Julia sat back, lifting her head. She said peremptorily, "Jon, sorry, I know you very well. We've worked together on countless charities that you personally spearheaded — the reading program for African refugees, the working mom support centers, the..." The defense was spilling out fast, the character evidence. "You have been an upstanding businessman, a fine citizen. You raised two wonderful sons. You're one of the most generous, kindest men I know."

"Julia, that's sweet of you," he said, invitingly patting the bed on the side near her. "But I was a different man. In my early twenties a lot had gone wrong. Really wrong. Was a drunk, a failure. My reputation as a bush guide was trash. Had nothing else going when this predator talked me into being part of his plan."

His three listeners waited respectfully for Jon to finish.

"Whatever the reason, however hard it is to believe, however it happened, it happened. I did it. What I did, the size of my sin, 'killed the moon.' That's what the San would say. I need to rebuild it."

Jon had said it. He visibly relaxed. He would have his peace.

"Now you've got enough. I'm tired. It's my money. Can use it how I want. Don't mean to be rude but fix this before I die. I'm not asking."

Jon winked at Julia to smooth over the tone of his directive, exhaled loudly and squeezed his eyes closed. With a trembling hand, he pulled on his sheet.

Julia did not move her head. Her eyes flicked from Jon's face to the morphine drip. Jon saw her through closed lids.

"No, Julia, it's not the drugs. It's my guilt. It's gotten too heavy."

Patrick, chair against the wall, could smell the coming war. By this point, he was sitting upright, leaning forward, hands clasped, elbows on his legs, eyes wide in disbelief.

Hunted humans? A deathbed change, giving everything to some Africans because he hunted their relatives. This, I haven't heard before.

Julia shook her hair, either because she had heard Patrick's thoughts or to get Jon to focus. Justin was still typing, getting everything that was said.

"All right, Jon, we need to go over this slowly." Here was the professional, the legal mind, the expert. "So, you and this man had volunteered to help protect farmers. Your acquaintance accidentally killed one San Bushman and the other survived. Those things happened back then, I imagine. We can identify heirs and other family to pay some damages. Let's start with what you know about them; names, where they lived, that sort of thing."

Jon persisted; his tone impatient. "The guy didn't accidentally kill a San. It was no accident. That's for sure. It was outright murder. He hunted them, me at his side, each step of the way, knowing what he was doing.

"I don't know their names. San Bushmen weren't like us. They didn't carry driver's licenses. No pockets, you know."

He laughed alone, the only one in the room to understand the joke.

"Only good part of this story, they killed him, killed that human hyena. Shot him with Bushman poison. Bad way to go.

"There was an inquest. You see, a white guy had been killed. The local authorities questioned me. I lied. Had to. The truth was he murdered a Bushman with me, his accomplice. They killed him in self-defense. I wasn't going to tell them *that*.

"Flew out of South Africa right away. Broke my father's heart to think I had volunteered for some right-wing band terrorizing innocent Bushmen. I hardly spoke with him before he died."

Jon's own time was coming quickly, he knew.

"This sin of mine, it shadows me. I have nightmares of creeping alongside that man, tracking the San like wild game. Hearing the gunshot.

"Since I came to America, I've watched your Klan, your lynchings, your police brutality. Those images, those struggles, they've kept my guilt raw.

"I thought, if you only knew. If you only knew what was done to the Bushmen… these peaceful human beings, scattered in the desert in small family groups — no marches, no powerful preachers, no civil rights lawyers. Just them in the desert. Treated like animals.

"My children and grandchildren are already rich. The families of these men aren't. They likely have nothing."

Jon rolled his eyes closed, inhaled deeply, and held it. He breathed weakly.

Julia waited for Jon to take a few breaths. "You don't know if these men had family, any descendants?"

"Not sure. Likely though. They all had families. Those families had families. Certain."

He raised a grey hand, blue veins pronounced. "Can you write up something to get this started, confirm what I want to be done with my money before I check out of here?"

"Does anyone in your family know about this, Jon?"

"About what? The hunt? My participation in the murder of a man whose only crime was being San. No. Never told anyone here. Did I tell them I'm changing my will? No."

Patrick saw Julia's back tighten.

Jon looked at her, then the others. He fixed on Patrick, the one man of color in the room. His brows lifted as if asking for Patrick's forgiveness.

"Being part of that hunt destroyed my relationship with my father. Maybe hurt him more than the war did. I loved that man. Putting these facts out there might be rough for my family. But I can't die without righting this."

He tried to roll over but managed only to weakly shift his weight and fall back. He groaned.

"Come back tomorrow."

His eyes closed, moving under grey lids, mouth open, now silent, but for wheezing. Patrick came to the bed, pulled a blanket up to his neck and tucked it around thin shoulders.

Julia stood by the bedside. "Patrick, you understand the importance of confidentiality." It was not a question.

"Yes, ma'am. I'll call when he's up for a visit tomorrow."

Chapter 4

Futile Conflict

Descending from Jon's floor, Julia studied the elevator lights as though they meant something. She and Justin were alone. She addressed him without turning her head.

"Start a list of legal issues from threshold to ancillary. I want Rogers from International part of the team. Let's also get Dr. Chodre on the line."

"Given his illness and medications," Justin reasoned, "I would think the first issue will be Chodre's assessment of Mr. Schmidt's capacity, right?"

Julia's narrowed eyes turned on him. With her phone she pointed toward the CCTV camera. St. Lawrence was high-end. 24-hour security teams monitored the elevators, with video and audio.

"Yes, *capacity*. If the hotel ballroom capacity can't take the whole group, we will find another."

Justin's shoulders rolled forward. He shrank into his dark tailored suit, realizing he had foolishly disclosed client confidential information.

Julia exited into the lobby while on her phone, not looking back at him. He followed, head down, sniffing, certain he could smell his future burning.

Early the next morning, sunshine lit mounds of bagels and fruit waiting for lawyers in the sixty-fifth-floor conference room of Cogswell & Worthy. Justin was first to arrive, having spent the night in the office preparing a briefing. He was hungry but left the food alone. He chose a seat facing the door, back to the wall.

Julia entered fast, as if pushing through a crowded New York sidewalk. She was rested, perfectly groomed.

Taking a seat across from Justin, she smiled at him for a second, frowned at her phone and asked without looking up, "So, where is he? Have you prepared a summary of where we are?"

He slid her a copy. She pulled it to herself by the tips of deep red nails, not her fingers.

Julia skimmed the headings on each page, then looked at her watch. As if on cue, Rogers rumbled in, his heavy frame filling the doorway as he did. Julia silenced her phone and turned it over, out of view.

"Rogers, good to see you."

He lifted his heavy cheeks in a half-smile and exhaled as he sat, apparently tired by the effort of walking in.

"Late last evening, Justin and I spoke with Dr. Chodre. When Mr. Schmidt was admitted to hospice, we retained her, a well-regarded psychiatrist, for just this sort of contingency. Frankly, though, this particular development is several orders of magnitude greater than what we usually see.

"Normally we have a last-minute bequest to an estranged love child, Vegas dancer kind of thing. Not a complete revision of a will due to guilt over, over… what he described. Not sure how we frame it. Murder? Accessory to murder? Conspiracy to commit murder? Crimes against humanity? Ethnic cleansing?"

There was a heavy weight in the room left by her questions. These were not legal topics ever before discussed in this conference room of Gogswell & Worthy or, for that matter, anywhere in the high-end Manhattan law firm.

She coughed lightly as if to clear the air, "Chodre met with Mr. Schmidt only a few days ago, as she does from time to time. She considers him to be of sound mind and quite capable. The cancer hasn't affected his mental functioning, except for fatigue. She ran him through questions on factual and ethical issues. He responded quickly and well.

"Her conclusion is that he is not impaired, save for the painkillers, the effect of which comes and goes. She'll testify to this, if we need her."

Justin saw her shoulders roll backward. She glanced at him, causing him to look down at the table. Nails on her right hand imperceptibly extended as she lifted her palm off the table.

Her voice lowered but was steady. "That's the good news," she declared, unconvincingly. "It's also the bad news. We have a client who wants to change his will because he participated in a murder and attempted murder, a hunt, of members of an African ethnic minority." She paused, having gotten the words out authoritatively and hearing them resound in the room. Her voice lowered. "We would've preferred his falling for a pole dancer."

"Justin, give us the high points of this Bushman business. Rogers, you have his memorandum for the details."

Justin straightened in his chair, his head still down.

He explained how Bushmen, often referred to as San people, were ancient inhabitants of the part of Africa where Jon had said he was hunting. They are some of the oldest people in what is called sub-Saharan Africa. They are distinct from other Africans. They are physically smaller, their skin is lighter, copper-colored, their eyes and facial features look Asian.

He looked across the table. Rogers put down his coffee to respond to an email on his phone, while thoughtlessly wiping Danish crumbs from his mouth with a forearm.

He doesn't care, thought Justin, careful to camouflage his disappointment. *But this representation means something, for once we have the chance to make a difference in this world! How could our lead international partner not see that, not even be curious?*

As a Yale freshman, Justin joined the student chapter of Amnesty international during his first week on campus. He chose courses on human rights and political and social challenges in Africa, majored in political science with an emphasis on the developing world — which taught him to do original research and even publish his senior thesis on labor unions in East Africa. But it was all books and no people. After graduation, his goal was to change that, to spend two years with Peace Corps in Africa, maybe teaching in Tanzania or Zambia.

He had grown up in Davenport, Iowa, the heart of the American heartland. His mother taught school and his father managed a small manufacturing plant. Their only child, Justin outwardly resembled the slight, short men on his mother's side of the family. He had her pale eyes and dark hair. But he had his father's character, expansive, even feisty.

A tall man with what he defended as a "heavy Midwestern build," his father was a forceful proponent of racial equality. He pioneered diversity hiring and mentorship at the plant. On the wall behind his desk, hung a black and white photo of Dr. Martin Luther King, Jr., under which he had written as a tribute, "Courage Knows No Color."

All his father's friends knew of Justin's plans to join the Peace Corps. He often threatened to retire early and join his son.

The summer of his third year at Yale all that was shattered. His father died of a heart attack on the job. At the cemetery, holding his mother's hand, Justin laid to rest his dream of making a difference in an East African village. He needed to stay in America closer to his mother and get on with his education and career. His father had left her alone and with only a modest retirement. Justin went straight to law school with the target of a well-paying law firm job on the East Coast.

Fate had relegated fulfilling work in Africa to the category of 'what could have been.' Jon Schmidt had just pushed it back into 'what could be.'

When Rogers stopped typing on his phone to reach for his coffee, Justin cleared his throat and carried on. His voice carried subtle determination, to push through the partner's indifference. "Their language is unique. It's full of clicks that are hard to imitate. Some San languages have over one hundred and fifty consonants. It's complex and anthropologists say it reflects an equally complex culture. There are dialects so different that some Bushmen can't understand each other."

He paused for a reaction. There was none.

His voice lowered and slowed. He explained how Bushmen were the indigenous people of the Kalahari. They were there before Black Africans migrated south from central Africa and Dutch settlers moved north from the Cape Colony in the 1600s.

"Dutch colonialists pushed inland, northwards, confronting, killing, and forcing indigenous San people further into the desert.

"San were literally, physically, caught in the middle, with stronger, well-organized African tribes migrating from the north and well-armed Dutch pressing up from the south."

Rogers wiped his mouth with the back of a fist, crumbs falling on the memorandum in front of him, already stained with coffee. His large face was flushed. Forcing a thick finger down his shirt collar, he gave it a tug as if to release pressure.

"Justin, as riveting as this is, I'm not aiming for a degree in anthropology or African history. Any chance you can get to what matters?"

Justin kept his calm. "Yes, sir. By 1955 and the time Mr. Schmidt entered South West Africa with his colleague, San had been forced north into poorer areas of the Kalahari, sort of like how we moved Native Americans onto reservations. White farmers were able to settle where San had historically been, in areas with better water and vegetation. These settlers were protected within what was called the Police Zone. San Bushmen and other Africans could not be in the zone unless they had authorization to work on a white farm or travel through.

"The area was geographically immense, starting on the Atlantic coast and moving inland all the way into Botswana. Think of it as larger than Kansas."

Rogers licked sugar off his fingers, hardly moved by a Midwestern boy's evocation of the size of one plains state or another. Nevertheless, he flipped to the map in Justin's memo.

"Police and military couldn't be everywhere. White settlers were given a lot of latitude in how they protected their livestock and farms. Often, they formed civilian militias to deal with cattle theft and other problems.

"Some South African authorities considered Bushmen feral, effectively sub-human. In most respects, the law offered them no protection.

"The idea that Bushmen were something other than fully human was not limited to South Africa. Well into the 1900s, several American anthropologists also postulated that they were sub-human. In 1925, the so-called 'Denver-African Expedition' from Colorado went to study Bushmen with the stated purpose of proving this hypothesis. The group's goal was to identify, and I quote, 'the real missing link between humanity and the lower animals.'"

Rogers reached for a bagel. Julia, for her part, was now attentively reading the memo.

He took a deep breath. "Local South African law reflected all this, with lethal results. I found a 2004 file from the United Nations High Commissioner on Refugees reporting that in 1936 South Africa, a relatively modern democracy at the time, allowed recreational killing of San men and women. Hard to imagine, but the report indicates that at least some authorities in South Africa allowed hunting and killing of these people by issuing a license for that purpose. A license for sport."

Julia winced at the word.

"I don't have more than this one UN report mentioning this. But even if I can't find another example or another source corroborating this report, this is obviously important. It shows that hunting of Bushmen is something that may have actually happened.

"The permit listed in the UNHCR file is said to have allowed hunting and killing of a Bushman, but only outside of South Africa itself, in the desert that is now Namibia. It was called "South West Africa" at the time. That is where Mr. Schmidt said he was. While legally distinct from South Africa, it was under South African control.

"All this is recent history. Bushman hunting and persecution happened during our client's lifetime." Justin paused to emphasize what he was about to say. "World War II started only *three* years after South African authorities issued this license."

He waited for a reaction. This time he got one.

"Are you saying," interjected Julia, "that a government authority in South Africa issued a license that allowed for the recreational hunting of a human being as late as 1936?"

"Yes." The Iowa boy had his audience. Rogers stopped chewing. "I don't have details of the license, but its issuance appears to be public record and…"

Julia cut him off. "We need to think about what that means for our client. You're right, Justin. This was during Jon's lifetime. He was born in 1932 at a time when, apparently, at least one government authority sanctioned, what do we call it, sport killing of Bushmen."

Justin sat up straighter with confidence. He still had more ammunition. "It might have gone on a bit longer. There is a reported application for a license to hunt and kill a Bushman in South West Africa, dated in 1937. That would mean that lawful, sanctioned, hunting of Bushmen might have continued until Jon was about five."

Rogers coughed. His small eyes shot sideways at Julia.

"Justin, if I could get a word in here." He did not wait for Justin to respond. "In a normal world, where the client wants a defense, this history of legal hunting might help. I understand how hunting of Bushmen, in limited circumstances, was allowed up through the mid-1930s, and maybe a little later. But, and it's a big 'but', the lawful, recreational killing stopped a full twenty years before the hunt Jon described.

"What was allowed in the 1950s when Jon said he and his partner went on their mission to protect white farmers was, I will put it in quotes, 'legitimate' self-help by farmers to protect livestock. A white farmer, alone or with a group, could take measures against Bushmen or other Africans who threatened their property. Sort of frontier justice. That's part of what Jon described.

"In foreign jurisdictions, as well as our own, when police or military overlook violence and crimes, you'll have violence and crimes."

He cleared his throat, turning his head left, right, and back, as if to relieve his neck of the head's weight. "Hypothetically, if someone, say Jon or his partner, just wanted to hunt a Bushman back then, that person could have done it under the pretext of protecting a farmer's cattle, pretending to be part of the volunteer militia.

"If he did that and, if in the process, he killed a Bushman, he would have had his human hunt — without concern that authorities would investigate.

"The point is," Rogers continued, but addressing only Julia, "Jon may well have been involved in what he described. But bad as this is, we might have a defense."

He repeated his earlier phrase, "At least we would in a normal world." Julia knew where he was going this time. "Our client would allow us — would be grateful for us — to defend this conduct by arguing that he wasn't there to hunt Bushmen. He was there to help respond to banditry, as did other responsible private citizens. They had an encounter with two Bushmen that went bad. That was unfortunate. But it's been sixty years. There are no witnesses or evidence. He wants to change his will to provide compensation for what went wrong."

Rogers was setting up to debate himself, something he loved doing.

"On the other hand," dramatically waving his arm, "if we argue that the killing was accidental and that Jon was there for a legitimate purpose, we're going to lose. One, it's not fully accurate and, two, and probably more importantly, Jon won't go for it. He wants to openly confess to having participated in this crime. He wants to admit what he did and state plainly that that's why he's changing his will. He's seeking penitence. For that, he needs to confess. Can't have one without the other."

Rogers moved to conclude with solemnity, "Hence, we are in a place with no standard defensive options that I can see."

The air conditioning whirred in the sixty-fifth-floor conference room. Julia shifted.

"We need a judo move out of this," said Justin, realizing as he said it, how presumptuous it sounded.

Rogers raised his eyebrows at Julia. She half-smiled back. He grunted to signal he was not done. He leaned forward against the conference table, a fleshy wrist pulling on his French cuffs. He tapped his Montblanc on Justin's memo in front of him.

"Judo and other martial arts aside, I want to underscore how dangerous this is from an international legal and, importantly, financial, point of view. Over the last forty years, public international law has developed to protect indigenous peoples and to punish perpetrators of genocide or racially based killings.

"If word got out about why Jon is changing his will — for example, in our papers filed with the court — then private citizens, here and abroad, could bring individual or class-action claims against the estate. We could expect suits to be brought by lawyers representing San or Bushmen or whatever you call them, indigenous peoples'advocacy groups, lawyers like David Boies, Amal Clooney or some other bounty hunter or crusader.

"If you doubt that, just ask Imelda Marcos. She and Ferdinand were sued everywhere. She managed to keep her shoes, but at a price.

"Misstep now and we drop the estate into years of litigation." It sounded almost tempting. "It'd be a prime-time, and very expensive, human rights drama."

His face reddening with the effort of this explanation, he pushed himself further forward, causing a portion of the table to disappear into his voluminous shirt. Enough of theory, it was time for an action plan.

"We need details," he barked. "Lots of details to assess risks. Jon reported that his companion and a Bushman were killed. If those were the only casualties, that's a good thing. But an inescapable component of our problem is that these Bushmen were apparently hunted because they were Bushmen. These men were targets of murder for no other reason than race, ethnicity. That might be a fatal infirmity in our defense of the estate." He paused before adding, "And of Jon."

Justin thought of the frail figure in the hospice bed. In an instant, he was called back to legal strategy, as Rogers continued,

"Other than knowing there will be litigation coming from all directions, there's no way to predict how this'll play out. If facts come out that Jon was part of a hunt of these people, the entire estate could be lost.

"We have to find a way to kill and bury this without litigation. Doing otherwise would be tantamount to malpractice."

Julia scowled without looking up. "Let's table for a moment the crimes against humanity, human rights and all that," she said, "and discuss timing. We know his children will sue immediately to stop us from changing the will. Would it be better if we battle his children while he's alive, so he can provide testimony, or after he passes, leaving his last word the last word?

"There's plenty of precedent for super rich making strange bequests. Leona Helmsley left $12 million to her dog. We aren't at that level of crazy.

"Jon's gift is unusual due to the motivation behind it, but leaving a fortune to set up a philanthropy in Africa is more normal than most. Serves the public good and all that. Would appeal to a court.

"The question I see is strategic; do we quietly build a file to defend the changed will after he is dead, or inform his heirs now and start the fight while he is alive?"

No one volunteered.

"Good. The decision is we stay quiet and learn more before lighting everything on fire."

Chapter 5

Declaration of War

A man fumed his way out of the lobby of St Lawrence, shouting into his cell phone. "Why have we never heard about this shit before?" he raged. "Hunted men!"

Jon had solved the timing problem for his lawyers by inviting his elder son, Gareth, to his hospice bed to declare war on the financial expectations of his firstborn.

Tan to a point of exaggeration, fit, hair too perfect, Gareth looked like the country club denizen he was. He took long, forceful strides toward a black Mercedes.

"We heard fifty times about every other fucking African hunt. But never this little adventure. Now what? Bushmen get everything?"

Folding himself into the backseat cushioned leather, he continued yelling at his lawyer with passersby catching most of what he said. He glared at them as he closed his door.

"Asked him who the man was, this Bushman. He didn't answer. I swear, doesn't fucking know. Get a shrink in there to confirm he's crazy. Holy shit, really? Hunted humans? He's delusional. You should've seen him, wheezing, waving his arms around, talking nonsense.

"Right goddamn now, I want you to draft papers to keep this maniac and Julia from making a deathbed change that screws everything."

He hung up and looked at nothing, his vision fogged by rage, able to see only the fortune he was losing. His driver kept his eyes forward.

"To the office."

"Yes, sir."

Gareth, partner in an investment banking firm, had taken time that morning from more important matters — that is, money. He had canceled a meeting and gone to St. Lawrence in response to his dying father's early morning call. It had been odder than most of his conversations with his father. Jon had been cryptic, saying only that he had to speak with Gareth that morning about his will. He would not say why.

Jon had never been comfortable with Gareth's love of money. For his part, Gareth was simply never comfortable with his father — not his hunting, his Africa complex, or anything else.

Gareth was born into privilege and, from the outset, spent his energies staying there — and becoming richer. Jon's decision to call Gareth to his bedside to tell him that his fortune was going to Bushmen had an obvious element of spite. It was a dagger stab at his eldest, made more acute because it involved Africa and charity. He knew Gareth liked neither.

Jon would wait a bit before talking with his other boy, Richard. He knew his youngest would like the idea of millions going to Bushmen, though he would be crushed when he learned why. It was going to be a difficult conversation.

Richard was ten years, almost half a generation, younger than his brother. He did not have his father's passion for hunting but effortlessly loved the African bush and people. He was small, like his father, with narrow shoulders, the same quick gait, and pale blue eyes.

He favored faded jeans, hair to his shoulders, and a t-shirt that advertised one liberal cause or another. Gareth referred to this as his brother's "leftist flowerchild" uniform.

Until his father fell ill, Richard and his father traveled frequently to Africa. Richard was in high school when he and his father made one of their many trips, this one to Selous Game Reserve in Tanzania.

Kneeling at elephant spoor one afternoon near their camp, Jon called his son over. "See how the feet are different shapes? The rear foot is more oblong, the front is round. The front, five toes, the back, four. Look at these ridges in the tracks. You can use those to follow a particular animal, they are like fingerprints."

Richard took several photos of the prints, examining them on his camera screen to better see the variations. "I think I can turn these into art," he said to his father.

"I expect you can. Now let's see if we can find this fellow to get him to pose for you before the sun sets."

That evening, Richard sat next to his father, who was chatting with their guide, Emmanuel, and several of the camp staff. While examining his photos of the day, he listened as his father excitedly discussed an education proposal he had come up with on the trip.

"I can start it out and have friends join me once we get it going," his father said. And turning to Emmanuel, "After we get back, send me photos and short statements from the young people you think are most promising. Let's do a mix of girls and boys for the scholarships. Total of ten, maybe. Secondary school. I have an old friend who teaches at Mohdri Boarding in Dar es Salaam. I'll give her a call."

Later that evening in their tent, Jon raised the project. "Son, it's not much. But it helps. Emmanuel told me how his oldest daughter is a strong student but likely will just get married and end her education. It's like that for all the girls and most of the boys in his village. That's when I had my idea. Need to develop this next generation of talent in Tanzania. It's a small step, but each one counts.

"Remember this, Richard, when you come here to Africa, you, like all of us, leave tracks. Make yours worth following."

Turning from his boy, he frowned and muttered to himself, "Some learn that too late."

Over many trips, Richard became his father's enthusiastic student, learning tracking and bush skills from him, as well as from African guides. Listening to stories of their lives, he often learned more about family and life than about the bush. Over the years, Richard fully absorbed his father's love of firelight, stars, as well as his passion for Africa.

Now, a young professional, he worked as a consultant for liberal candidates who, as Gareth snarked, "probably don't even play golf." In his brother's opinion, Richard wallowed in mediocrity, working for socialists, Democrats, who wanted everyone, everything, to be mediocre. Gareth rarely spoke with him.

This morning in New York, however, Gareth, unfortunately, had no choice but to call his sibling. He got an annoyingly chirpy voicemail message telling him to leave a message and have a spiritually fulfilling day.

"Rick, dad's having a moment, a major moment. We need to talk ASAP. Give me a shout."

He'll love the idea of deathbed penance, even if dad's insane.

An hour later, Gareth paced back and forth along the floor-to-ceiling windows of his midtown office, slapping his phone against his thigh in frustration. He looked again at his Rolex. Impatient, he called his attorney.

"Paul, it's been hours," he snapped. "I expect a temporary restraining order to freeze the will as it is, a motion for sanctions against Cogswell & Worthy, and a complaint to the New York Bar about Julia."

"Ready to go, Gareth."

"Shoot them straight off to Julia. Copy me and, I suppose, Richard. No word from him. He's probably at a protest somewhere. We can't wait. Let's get Julia squirming as soon as we can. She might step back."

Julia was downing her seven-p.m. espresso when she got Paul's demand,

Julia,

Please find attached papers that we will file immediately, absent assurance on your part that you will take no action in support of Mr. Schmidt's alleged deathbed request to alter fundamentally and unlawfully his last will and testament.

Our filing seeks a temporary restraining order until a third-party expert has completed a full assessment of Mr. Schmidt's mental capacity. New York law allows for this relief due to Mr. Schmidt's substantial medical issues and level of medication.

In parallel, we intend to request sanctions for breach of ethical duties against you personally and your firm. On information and belief, you and your firm have encouraged and enticed Mr. Schmidt to consider these changes. By this, you are self-dealing and taking advantage of an elderly, incapacitated client. That conduct warrants sanctions, to include our fees and costs, as well as damages for the pain and suffering you have inflicted on Mr. Schmidt's family.

It is the view of a family member that you have manipulated Mr. Schmidt for your own gain. Your

conduct, as such, violates multiple rules of professional conduct that protect clients and their families from this sort of predatory practice. Accordingly, also attached is a draft complaint we intend to file with the Bar of New York that seeks sanctions against you personally, to include disbarment.

Please let me know if you would like to discuss a resolution and mutually acceptable settlement.

Respectfully,
Paul Leveque, Esq.

Large caliber rounds had just been fired, hitting the dirt at her feet. Calmly putting down her small cup, she summoned Justin and dialed Leveque on her speakerphone.

"Paul, how *have* you been? I trust your wonderful family is doing well." Her voice was warm syrup. "Listen, I got your papers. Thanks for sending them over. Are you available? I could be in your offices in about thirty. Looking over what you say here, I think we can work something out."

"That would be fine. Should I invite Gareth and Richard?"

"Please."

Moments later, Gareth's phone buzzed during his dinner. He held a finger to his ear to hear Paul over the restaurant noise.

"Good news, she responded right away. Wants a meeting tonight. I think the draft ethics complaint may have shaken her. Probably not her first. She might not want another."

"I'll be there by eight," Gareth replied, adding with dismissive sarcasm, "alone. Shockingly, Rick hasn't gotten back to me. He's seemingly out of range, probably on a Greenpeace boat chasing some tuna fishermen. We'll leave him out of this for now."

Meanwhile, Julia, after hanging up with Paul, calmly stood and gracefully swung her briefcase over a shoulder.

"You've got a passport?" she asked Justin. It sounded more like an instruction.

"Yes. At home. Why?"

She ignored his question. She was on her phone calling a driver. Justin followed behind her, seeing that her calves were sharply defined as if she was springing with her steps. Her shoulders straightened, pulled down and back. He looked down to stay seemingly unaware of the physical energy she appeared to be preparing to launch.

Once in their town car, she looked up at the sky through the moon roof, catching it between the cliffs of Midtown. She tapped the glass,

"Justin, look at that."

Justin silently looked up. All he could see was New York.

She kept her gaze aloft. "Jon would say a full moon is perfect for hunting."

Part II

African Origins

Chapter 6

Star Hunter

Roots of the legal conflict in New York extended back a lifetime deep into the soft sand of the Kalahari, to a place just north of the Orange River. There, four members of a Bushman family felled an eland. It was sometime in the 1930s.

They had waited silently, tucked into brush, using a full moon as bait. It shone low on the horizon to their right, a beacon, pulling the massive antelope on a line that would cross in front of them.

The four hunters were all from the same family. They worked well together, having played, and hunted with each other their whole lives. These men had been schooled by the same elders, one of whom led the hunt.

None was over five feet tall. Each wore a quiver of arrows and a loincloth of springbok skin, nothing else. They were silent, bent over, becoming even smaller than usual, moving with easy steps on the sand. Their copper skin helped them disappear into shadows as they found a place downwind of where the eland would walk. Only the soft springbok leather they wore made any sound at all, a faint swishing, as their legs moved gracefully around thorn bushes, their small feet landing noiselessly.

Hunting was serious business but done with pleasure. The men's near-constant smiles compressed almond-shaped, seemingly Asiatic, eyes that laughed silently above high cheekbones.

Elands are enormous. This quarry was four times heavier than all the hunters combined. For the small men peering through foliage, half-light from the moon made the eland seem bigger than he was. Crouched in the shadow of squat mopane, they could make out details of the beast, moonlight putting in sharp relief his large neck and shoulder muscles. They could see them move rhythmically when he tossed his head, pulling branches, jaws working, walking with a confidence that his size and speed provided.

The four hunters knew that this eland, like other browsers, would walk toward the setting moon. Lunar light provided both a celestial lure and a means of targeting him. The moon and starlight illuminated the beast from above, as well as from below since the pale sand reflected the light. The dual lighting sharpened his profile, rendering him distinct, even in the dim of the night.

A weak wind blew from him to them. The men sniffed, catching a faint odor of prey.

For his part, the eland could not smell them. Unaware of the danger, he moved steadily from a copse of trees toward an opening of starlit sand. In a few steps, he would expose himself for enough time.

As he lumbered forward onto the lit soil, the hunters, on a silent signal from the elder, pulled back on their seemingly miniature bows. Simultaneously they launched four arrows. Small, unfletched, no more than sharply pointed sticks, they flew silently in a gentle arc, landing at the same time.

A potent poison made from orange and black leaf beetle larvae covered each arrow tip. Slight penetration of the animal's hide with the toxin — that is all they would need to bring down this eland bull of almost two thousand pounds.

One of the four arrows stuck into the top of the bull's haunches. As he darted off, the arrow dislodged, falling like a toy into the brush. The men excitedly trotted over, slowing to find their arrows. Once they collected the lethal projectiles and placed them carefully in quivers, they got on their hands and knees. With the benefit of the moon, starlight, and their child-sized, light fingers, the hunters analyzed the hoof prints of their prey.

The oldest and the smallest whispered to the others, "See how his left front turns in. If he crosses other tracks or runs with others, we'll find him."

Wordlessly, the younger men bent over dark grey imprints left by the fleeing eland, taking slow lunges forward, eyes down. The hunters memorized how the beast moved, the size, shape and spacing of his hooves. They focused on his left front foot which left distinctive spoor.

Moving easily through the bush, they paced themselves as a group now jogging after the bull which, alarmed by the hit of the arrow and the men behind him, was running much faster than they toward the setting moon.

It was going to be a long run, but the bull would die. He was theirs.

It took that night and the rest of the next day. They found the eland toward dusk, exhausted, dying, breathing heavily, eyes large in fear. Squatting near him, the men were silent.

After a respectful period, the oldest hunter spoke, the others remaining quiet. He softly said to the bull, "We shall honor you. We shall bring our families to you, to live where you give us life."

He turned to the youngest of the hunters. This young San, his hair almost shaven, held himself with a young man's energy, taught, upright. Xhabbo was fast, the older hunter knew. He also knew that this young man would want to go back to the family. His wife was pregnant and likely to give birth any day.

Referring to the extended family in the first-person plural, the elder asked the young man, "Can you go and bring us here?"

He did not have to add, "be quick." There was one speed in the bush; what could be managed. If a San were thirsty and hungry, he would walk slowly to conserve his energy to reach his goal. If he was fit and rested, as was Xhabbo, he would trot.

Bow in his left hand, the young father-to-be ran lightly, his feet hardly leaving traces in the sand. Against his dark brown back, a hard, natural cylinder held four arrows. Made of a quiver tree branch, capped with animal skin, it fit well against his back, clapping gently as he ran.

Noshay will be pleased with this hunt. She is large with our baby. The eland and the moon might make our son come see me.

While Xhabbo wove through a maze of bushes and trees back toward where they had left the family several days earlier, the three remaining hunters began skinning and preparing the eland. Soon enough, his meat hung from branches, in strips, drying in the hot wind, marking the place where he died.

In this way, the eland, "dhoo" in this family's language, would give Qxatta his birthplace.

Xhabbo rejoined his family during the night. It had been a silent reunion with his pregnant wife. She had felt him near her, his heat, his smell. When he folded on the sand beside her, she glanced his way but turned her eyes back to watch the darkness, as would any expecting mother in the bush. A moment after he lay down, she heard him breathing deeply. She exhaled, closed her eyes for a moment and then, again opened them to watch the night.

One hand on her abdomen, she turned to Xhabbo's form in the darkness. The baby moved. She smiled.

He knows his father is here. He is already a hunter, my baby boy. I feel him hunting more and more at night, even when you are sleeping, my husband. This boy hunts with the stars.

At dawn, the family began the trek to the eland. It would take several days. Neither she nor anyone else in the family gave any thought to her late-stage pregnancy. San women, even ready to deliver, continue to gather and prepare food, care for younger children, build shelter, and move with their families.

Xhabbo initially led the family group. By mid-morning, he fell back to walk near Noshay. He knew that other Bushmen family members walking in front could easily follow his footfalls through the desert to the eland.

Smiling broadly at her he said, "He was a grandfather eland. As tall as two of me. One arrow hit him on his back. We were hunting quietly, in the shadows, he did not see us. His horns, this big," he gestured with his arms fully extended over his head.

Smiling, she glanced down at the sand in front of her. She could see his toe prints, his smooth heel, the regular, light crescent moon tracks he left in the sand as he walked in front of her.

Hand under her belly, she spoke to her baby, *Look, my son. Walk lightly as your father walks.*

She paused at an acacia tree with white thorns to pull off pearls of gum Arabic oozing at joints where branches met the trunk. She quickened her steps to catch up to Xhabbo. The gum provided no nutrition, but it comfortably wet her mouth as she chewed.

With sunset the next day, they came to where the eland had died. All afternoon, the wind had been blowing toward them from the camp, allowing her to smell rich smoke from the meat. It warmed her, even from a distance.

The first thing she saw were strips of meat high in the bushes and trees. As they got close, she could see that at ground level there were several small, rounded huts. They smelled new, inviting, made of fresh grasses and branches. Between them, two fires smoked in the sunlight.

Her father, Toma, squatted on his heels at one of the fires roasting dark brown 'kquee 'nuts, rolling them with a stick. Without pausing his cooking, he turned his eyes to her. Deep creases cut shadows over his smile.

"Welcome, my Noshay."

She stopped and stood awkwardly for a moment, as if trying to keep her balance. Xhabbo came to her side.

"Rest with your father."

Noshay's father pushed some 'kquee' nuts from the coals. He struck them each, hard, with a stick to break them open. He offered them to her in a yellow and black tortoiseshell bowl.

She sat close to him while she ate the warm nuts, resting on an elbow, allowing sun-heated sand to support her back and belly. Daughter smiled broadly at father, her eyes all but disappearing above dark cheeks. Content and safe with family, Noshay fell asleep.

As she dozed, her nephew, Toushay, toddled over. He was only two, but already moving easily around the camp. He carefully skirted the fires and backed into his grandfather's lap. Looking at his aunt, he furrowed his brows. He leaned toward her, out of his grandfather's lap, to wave off flies near her face. He used his small hands to smooth the sand near her head. Falling back into his grandfather's lap, he was treated to a nut. Chewing slowly, the boy closed his eyes, his back against Toma's bare chest.

Noshay napped only a short while. She woke as shadows filled the camp, the sun well behind thickets. She got up easily and joined several men and women preparing the eland hide. They worked together, scraping it clean, rubbing it with their hands, working in fat and chatting.

As the night cooled, they ate, their bellies protruding and the eland's energy moving from the antelope to the family. Full, they celebrated. With bare feet shuffling in the sand, the men made a large oval around the two fires, dancing to honor the hunt and to welcome the night sky full of other hunters.

Xhabbo and Toma acted out the hunt with exaggerated drama. Toma was the wise eland, wary and careful, and Xhabbo, leading the other hunters silently, with respect, pretended to follow the beast from a distance, unseen.

Without warning, Xhabbo abruptly shouted as they danced around the fire, "Look, Grandfather, the moon, your moon!"

Noshay's father, in character of the eland, turned his head up, looking where Xhabbo pointed, his thin outstretched arms imaginary eland horns turning toward the light.

Noshay sang and clapped with them. From time to time, she looked away from the fire, craning her neck to see into the night sky.

Maybe my son will come when he sees his star.

Hours later, she lay in one of the huts, enveloped by the sweet smell of drying grass. On her back, she watched the night sky move through a lattice of branches and grasses that made her domed ceiling. Hyenas whooped close by. The sound of an animal scurrying by the fire was too light for a hyena. Protectively, she nevertheless placed two hands on her belly.

Only a jackal.

Pushing her head back, she studied the shards of night sky visible through the hut's branches.

Son, he will come, your star.

Jackal, I hear you still nosing cold coals. There's no food for you.

She exhaled, her stomach rising.

Are you listening, my son? No lions or leopards tonight. Birds are quiet. They would tell us.

There he is, pointing at the sky low behind her head.

Look, son. Your star. See him hunting slowly, climbing the sky? We can't see his prey, but he can. He hunts silently, like your father.

Her baby moved slightly, as if answering.

Yes, you see it don't you?

Noshay lay watching the star as it passed out of sight behind a branch and then became visible again in a wedge sky. She felt her baby responding as the star moved.

It is time.

She got up without waking her husband or anyone.

But her older sister, Nisa, heard her from her adjacent hut. Nisa quietly, lithely, bent through her hut's low door, picked up a spear and followed.

The butchered eland had attracted hyenas that now nosed around in the bush, usually just outside the firelight. With the fires out, they were closer. Noshay could smell them and hear their breathing, sniffing, grunting. She also heard seemingly insane yelps, and whoops from those further out in the bush. With two women standing outside their huts, the jackal abandoned where he had been digging near a fire and skittered into the night.

Hearing him run from camp, Noshay thought, *Good. Go. Go tell your hyena cousins. They're to leave me alone.*

She did not speak to her sister who was standing in the dark to her side. She did not have to, nor did she want to. This was her time and her son's time.

Her back to the huts, Noshay's eyes swept the dark bush in front of her and the millions of hunters above. She could hear the muffled movement of Nisa's springbok leather behind her as they walked away from the huts to find a birthing place. The soft sound of Nisa was all the comfort she needed.

She found a spot, shaded from starlight by a short apple leaf tree. There, she squatted silently, one hand on the tree's trunk.

I can feel you, my son. I hear you, too.

Through silent pain, she glanced up through overlapping leaves, finding the star. Head lowered; she bore down. She inhaled when looking up again at the sky. Again, and again.

Her eyes, ears, nose, were all alert for danger. Nostrils sought the scent of predators. Eyes bore into the bush, looking for movement.

Pain caused her eyes to compress. The pressure filled them with light. She opened them, focusing again, tears falling silently through the dust on her cheeks.

The young woman exhaled and took a deep breath, making almost no noise. Her hand gripped the tree. She felt a magnified sensation of the rough bark in her hand, the sand, and leaves under her feet. Every sense was on edge.

I hear you, Nisa. I hear you behind me, to my side, in front of me.

Nisa circled slowly, carrying her thin spear, watching, listening, smelling, determined to protect her sister when the scent of the baby's birth would be carried by the wind into the trees and bush. As soon as they caught the smell, lions, leopards, wild dogs, and hyenas would follow it to the infant.

I know, Noshay, this is your night. Your boy is coming. Hyenas are close. They know it too. They'll smell me, see me, and stay back.

Noshay watched as stars rose and fell. She bore down, pushing, her son's star moving up and now beginning its descent, hunting still. Silently, she delivered her child. Exhausted, wet with sweat and blood, she smiled as she felt he was a boy — just as she knew the baby would be.

Nisa, spear in hand, trailed a few paces behind her, back to the huts. Neither had spoken. Hyenas had remained at a distance, even when the air was thick with the smell of birth. Such was the strength of her sister's protective presence.

Back in her shelter, Noshay lay on her back. Again, a million hunters flickered above her, showing themselves briefly through gaps in the thatching. She sought one among them all.

She cupped her son's head as he nursed. His soft hair, miniature feathers in her palm. She did not look at him. Instead, she watched the heavens through the lattice.

There it is. It has finished hunting for the night. It is coming down to rest. Your star is ready for you, my boy.

Holding her baby, she left the hut. The persistent jackal who had returned to his scavenging, scampered again into the dark.

Thank you, jackal, for telling your cousins to stay away tonight. I'll leave you something tomorrow.

She stood near one of the fires that still smoked lightly from the night before. She dug her toes into warm sand under the coals. Her shoulders back, she lifted the newborn so that he was between her and his star. She held him at arm's length, waiting for the celestial hunter to fill her son.

I can see it in you, feel it in you, my son. Carry this star, this hunter, in your heart.

Born and blessed where the "dhoo" had given his life and his wild energy to the family, Qxatta, as he was named, lived a childhood rich with love. It was the love of every adult, every larger child, lifting, carrying, and caring for him. Swaddled naked in the warmth of parents, aunts, uncles, cousins, grandparents, Qxatta never touched the ground without the protection of a watchful member of his family. As his eyes opened and could focus in his first few months, his first sights were of the back of the relative carrying him, leaves or thorns through which they walked, fires dancing at night, and movement of the sun and the stars, the millions of stars.

Of everything in his world, the stars held his gaze.

One evening when he was about six months old, Noshay gently put Qxatta down on a piece of eland hide, as she often did. She tucked the edges around him to keep him warm. She had placed him just outside of the firelight to make the stars clearer for her baby.

Watching him for a minute, she turned to her husband laughing, softly clapping her hands for his attention. "Xhabbo, look at your son. Look how he is again finding his hunting star. Quiet, happy, waiting for his star to rise, like he does each night."

Qxatta's older cousin, Toushay, came to lie next to him. Toushay doted on Qxatta, often putting a pudgy arm around him, or smoothing the sand near his head, as he had for Noshay on the eve of Qxatta's birth. On this night, Toushay brushed clean the sand around Qxatta.

He said with the assurance of a toddler, "See, Qxatta, I keep you safe. Nothing can crawl to you."

He lay down next to Qxatta, their heads close, Toushay's small hand in dark profile against the night sky, a finger pointing up. He whispered, "They hunt like Grandfather, silently."

Qxatta grew up in a world of family, in a nursery of bush and sky. He walked by eleven months. On that day, after taking his first tentative side to side steps, he was scooped up in the laughing embrace of Xhabbo, who held him proudly above his head, announcing that his son was walking. Toushay was at his side clapping and dancing in the dust.

Hunger and thirst marked many days for the family. One day, still too young to walk far on his own, he was on his mother's back as the family moved to where his grandfather thought they would find water and game. Qxatta rode his mother's hip easily, used to her rhythm, watching the bush go by, acacia trees, thorns of all sizes, tall grasses.

They stopped to rest in the late afternoon. The family had not had water in several days. The adults were moving slowly. They chatted quietly as they settled in shade.

Qxatta, free from his mother, ran, as he could, after Toushay, in grasses as tall as the boys. After a few minutes of play, Toushay heard a whimper, not a cry, and turning around could not see his cousin. A few steps behind him, the toddler was on his back holding his right foot in the air. From it protruded a short portion of a leadwood tree branch, its thorns long and hard. Several had penetrated Qxatta's bare foot.

Tears left wet traces in the dust on his face. He was silent, though his lips trembled.

Toushay reacted confidently, mimicking adults in the family. He pushed against Qxatta's foot, pulling the small branch away. Neither boy said a word. Qxatta did not cry out. Nor did Toushay dishonor his cousin by comforting him or calling for help. Pain was part of their lives. Withstanding it wordlessly was part of growing up.

In the week to come, infection and fever set in.

"Hold his foot in the smoke," his grandfather said as Qxatta's grandmother stirred the fire with the leaves of a medicinal plant.

Noshay held her son, who shook in her arms.

"His star is fading," Noshay replied.

Qxatta's grandmother said, "No, it's poison from the thorns."

The old woman held the narrow last six inches of an oryx horn close to the coals. She scooped ashes of the leaves into the horn. While it was smoking, she placed it under Qxatta's largest puncture wound, gently pressing it against the foot until the horn cooled. She repeated the process with the other puncture wound.

For several weeks, one family member or another carried Qxatta. His grandmother repeated the oryx horn treatment several times. Toushay rarely left his side, often poking Qxatta to get a smile.

By the time the infrequent rains came that year, Qxatta had healed. But his illness had left a mark. His right leg was left weaker than the other, slightly smaller and turned inwards.

One afternoon when crossing open, hot sand, the boys trailed the family, looking into holes and tracking birds. Qxatta's father was behind them to ensure that the young boys more or less followed the others.

Toushay jumped onto a large, deep red volcanic rock that broke out of the sand between the boys and the family. He surveyed the Kalahari from his perch of several feet. Qxatta joined him, pushing him off center.

Toushay laughed, "Look back at your prints. See your right foot? I can. It is smaller than the other one, it turns in. I could track you at night with my eyes closed."

Qxatta knew he limped and that his right leg was smaller than his left. His eyes following their track back toward Xhabbo, Qxatta could see his footprints standing out among all the others.

Hopping off the rock, he ran to a bush, broke off a branch and jogged back over his tracks. Walking backward in an exaggerated fashion, with the branch dramatically sweeping the sand behind him, he backed onto the rock.

"Now, you can't see me."

He shoved Toushay off the rock.

"And now I can't see you."

The laughing boys trotted to keep up with the family.

Chapter 7

Black Death

Among steel and glass towers of Manhattan, in a world Bushmen in the 1930s could not have imagined, lawyers armed with iPhones and laptops accessing cloud-based search engines prepared for combat. As they postured for advantage, what remained of Jon's weak body was withering. The cancer was taking more and more of him. Thin white hair lay in lifeless wisps on a pink head resting on a pillow. The old man's eyelids pressed shut in pain. Eyes rolled rapidly beneath them, left and right, panicked. Light blue lips emitted barely audible words.

Patrick could only hear a faint "no" and, perhaps an African name, "Msizi," repeated before Jon's mumbling stopped altogether.

Thin arms jerked under the sheets. Skeletal legs tried weakly to lift against the bedding. Patrick could see he was in a nightmare, one of his frequent ones, dark and violent.

Mr. Schmidt, I can't make your dreams better, but I can make you more comfortable.

He adjusted Jon's drip and injected a dose of hydromorphone through the IV lead. The narcotic took Jon, relaxing his limbs, eyes, and mouth, dropping him back into jolting memories of a hunt gone terribly wrong.

A beast that needed water, lots of it, lifted its muzzle to the wind, ears flicking. His black nose glistened, dripped. Large eyes bulged with anxiety as jaws worked the cud in his mouth, drops of green spilling over black lips. He was alone, this Cape Buffalo bull. Not able yet to hear or smell the threat, he nevertheless sensed that danger was near.

The beast left the water and curled slowly to his right, to ambush whatever was trailing him. He walked deliberately, unhurriedly. He had done this before. One after the other, his large black hooves quietly compressed grasses as he moved. He lowered his head, weaving it left and right, sweeping at a cloud of flies that pestered him. Wet vegetation hung from his black horns. This dagga boy was on the hunt for whatever was hunting him.

Hours before, when preparing to hunt this bull, Msizi had been uncharacteristically quiet.

Under the morning's flat sky, Jon offered him a steaming mug of coffee. The Zulu sat on a log several meters from the small fire. His long legs stretched almost to the coals. As he sipped, the sky above him lightened, transitioning low clouds from dark grey to red.

Jon's hand rested for a second on Msizi's shoulder. He had seen him staring into the coals as if trying to see something.

"You good, mate?" Jon asked.

"Feeling a bit off, that's all. Thanks."

"Any news from home? All good with my namesake?"

"All good. When Percy drove in yesterday, he told me that little Jon walked for the first time. I should have been there. We both should have."

"My Zulu godson, already on the hunt? You're right. We must get back right fast!" he said, slapping Msizi's shoulder. "Let's get this dagga boy. His head's going home as a gift to your boy. A fitting tribute to this young Zulu warrior."

Msizi smiled at Jon.

I love you, brother. I swear, there is a Zulu hidden in your white body somewhere.

Jon poured his coffee on the fire and kicked dirt on it. "Let's get that dagga boy trophy for our little Jon."

Late that afternoon, heat enveloped them, as Jon led Msizi on the spoor of the lone bull. Several paces behind, still uneasy from the morning, the Zulu was increasingly anxious. Jon sensed it and looked back at him. Msizi furrowed his brows.

Jon don't turn your head to me. Stay focused. I should be leading. This boy is close. I can feel it.

A crack to their left stopped both men. Crouching, they scanned the low bush for a dark leg or tail or movement. Nothing. They stood and moved slowly forward, both certain the bull was close.

A branch now snapped on the right, followed quickly by another breaking loudly. Jon swept his rifle across his chest to his right shoulder, levering in a round as he did. He took a step forward with his left foot, poised for the shot. Msizi did the same.

They waited. Only buzzing insects broke the quiet. Msizi and Jon reflexively controlled their breathing, taking their breaths almost in tandem, their eyes the only part of them moving, scanning left, right, to the ground and up a meter, looking for movement, for a charge.

It came at Jon. The bull crashed through scrub, horns hooking back and forth. At an angle to the rushing buffalo, Msizi had an open shot at the bull's lower shoulder — but waited.

This is Jon's trophy.

Jon steadied. He sighted the bull straight on, the beast's head a rocking, black pendulum of death. It closed straight in on him.

Come to me. That's it. Give me a chest shot, I don't want to have to repair your head.

Abruptly, as if hearing Jon's thoughts, the dagga boy slammed four hooves into the dust and spun back into the bush.

Jon lowered his rifle. "Damn."

Branches snapped and then the bush quieted again. Msizi gestured to Jon.

He's hunting us now.

Msizi signaled to Jon that the bull was to their right. They heard crashing, tracking the noise with their rifles as it moved past them on the right side. A minute later there was no sound of the two-thousand-pound old man, only the hum of flies and the quiet, controlled breathing of the hunters.

Jon pointed down the trail, gesturing.

There is a break ten meters up. Let's get out of this tight bush.

Msizi looked over his shoulder as he stepped forward after Jon. Every part of the young Zulu was on edge, every part of him straining to hear or feel the buffalo.

He'll come back.

The charge took Msizi on his weaker side, his left, the side that required him to spin fully around to get a shot. It was as if the beast knew how to hunt the man. Msizi pivoted at the sound, raising his rifle.

Jon twisted as well.

It took them both too long.

"Msizi! No!"

"Mr. Schmidt, it's OK. I'm here. It's just a dream," Patrick said, gently holding Jon's shaking shoulders still against the bed.

Without opening his eyes, in a whisper Patrick could barely hear, Jon said, "It happened so fast. Msizi shot it, but that black monster was running on fury, hooked him deep, and with a twist of his powerful neck threw him high into the air. I shot the bastard several times."

Jon coughed.

"I didn't take the shot when I could've. My mistake. My dearest friend twisted on the ground. Opened. I could see his guts. His head, his head, I held in my lap. Like this."

Jon cupped his hands over the blanket, unable to control their tremors.

Translucent, silver tears formed trails running down either side of Jon's face, interrupted only by grey stubble as they curled to his neck. He closed his eyes.

"Patrick, listen to me, to an old man dying... " He wanted to set a conclusion solidly into the room. "I didn't realize it for years to come, but most of me bled out there in the dirt with Msizi, my brother."

Chapter 8

Nocturnal Predator

Julia was on her own hunt, Justin at her side. Carried in deep, black leather seats, hidden behind smoked glass, the two crossed Midtown. Their hired town car passed in and out of dark shadows created by skyscrapers that broke the bright moonlight into shards of black.

Arriving at Paul's office, Julia entered the conference room as if it were her territory. The moon, full and low in the sky, was now exposed in its entirety down a long canyon of buildings. It became a spotlight that penetrated the room's exterior wall. It illuminated the lawyers and their field of battle.

"Paul, so good to see you," she said extending a hand. "Gareth, you're looking well." She offered Gareth her hand. He took it more slowly than had Paul.

Tossing her hair, bright green eyes locked on Gareth, she asked, "Will Richard be joining us?"

Paul answered to draw her attention from his client to himself, "Not tonight. Julia, let's get started, shall we?"

Sitting poised, her back not touching her chair, she extended her chin. Her voice was steady, her cadence measured.

"Your shot over our bow was premature. We recommend you step back and let us do our work. File these papers and you," she looked at Gareth, "and your brother will likely never see a cent of this estate. It'll be trapped in litigation, chewed away by lawyers, while your family's reputation gets wrecked."

Paul raised a hand to keep Gareth quiet. "Julia, we see straight through your threat. Your firm stands to earn substantial fees managing Mr. Schmidt's new idea of a foundation. Or you get rich fighting this with us. Conveniently, you win either way — that is, unless we prevail.

"Our filing, in the public docket, will chronicle your misconduct. Our complaint with the New York Bar won't be public, but it will be as comprehensive. Taking advantage of an incapacitated, elderly client — you face suspension from practice."

Julia smiled benignly as if Paul were a waiter bringing a drink.

"Here is why," she said slowly, in a lowered voice, articulating each word, "you will do nothing."

Her eyes were narrow slits aimed at Gareth.

"Your father is mentally capable. He's admitting to multiple crimes for which there's no statute of limitations — they never become time barred. Those include premeditated murder, attempted murder, crimes against humanity, ethnic cleansing." The four arrows hit their target. Gareth straightened defensively. She added, "Not most people's idea of African game hunting.

"File your papers and breaking headlines will read, 'Deathbed Confession of NYC Philanthropist, 'I Hunted Humans.'

"Forget his life of charity work, forget his dedication to Africa. Instead, he'll be transformed into a monster — in a league with the worst racists we know. In the eyes of your peers, the public, and your clients, your father will join James Earl Ray, the two of them, rifles in hand. Or maybe Bull Connor and his dogs, Nathan Forrest, and his flaming crosses.

"Worse still, he can't be cast as a racist with a deluded but perceived 'noble purpose' — protecting a dying way of life, preserving the Old south or anything romantic like that. He was out there, part of a self-appointed militia, illegally planning to track down and persecute Bushmen. It turned into a hunt of humans, for nothing more than recreation, for sport. Instead of an elephant or rhino, the game? Innocent men.

"Now he wants penance, absolution. He wants to confess and make things right.

"File your papers and we'll have no choice but to respond by detailing what he's told us, to give the court an understanding of the magnitude of the issues, the nature of his crimes and the depth of his repentance. Our filing, like yours, will be in the public docket.

"In no time, more New York lawyers will pick up the scent. They'll inform the governments of South Africa and Namibia of his confession, offering to sue the estate on contingency. That's right, they'll work for free, up until the victims are compensated and then they'll get their cut. As if by coincidence, they'll claim damages that amount to, well, the entire fortune. There are San Bushmen communities in both countries. Those communities could put their share of the $100 million to good use.

"Those enterprising lawyers will be joined by others from various UN agencies, suing the estate, seeking compensation for gross human rights violations. There will be TV appearances, celebrity lawyers preening…"

Paul tried to cut in, "Julia, you can't…"

"You're the one who threw knives on the table. Let me finish.

"These won't be hard cases to litigate, will they?" she continued. Both Paul and Gareth huffed and sat up to show resolve. She only shook her head, as if teaching a lesson to mere boys. "The defense folds — on day one. Jon wants nothing more than to confess."

She didn't need to echo Rogers's admonition, "We're not in a normal world." They could see for themselves.

"Jon wants nothing more than to give his money away. The fight, if there is any at all, will only be about how the estate is divvied up between Bushmen, African governments, and the lawyers. While that's going on, you two brothers will be busy trying to explain to your neighbors, family, and clients how your father is any different from a Nazi war criminal.

"Attack my firm and me? Nothing but a predictable attempt to deflect from the horror that led Jon to confess. I know journalists who would love to take this story, about how our firm tried to help Jon do the right thing, make reparations to this poor African minority."

Paul hissed, "Your threats show how desperate…"

She raised a hand and looked only at Gareth. "Jon's not dead, and neither are you and Richard. But in twenty-four hours your reputations might be. They will be gone with your chance at inheritance."

She touched her lovely hair, gently.

"Gareth, I know your children love their grandfather. As they grow up, they should be proud of his legacy, a legacy that will be theirs. Don't make it a legacy of shame."

Justin could see Gareth turning red. Paul was going white.

"Your dad, lying in his hospice bed, has dreams of hunts," continued Julia softly. "Some seem real, others not. So, here's what we'll do for you to keep this quiet," she said, now almost in a dramatic whisper. "To see if there's a chance that Jon is delusional. To find a way to fix this." Now that they were listening intently. She had them. She delivered the prize, "We'll find out what happened."

Justin leaned forward. He needed to make sure he got every word.

"Agree not to file and Justin is on the next flight to Cape Town to find out if Jon did what he said he did and, if so, to get police records, find witnesses. Or to determine there is no support for his story. One way or another, pray your dad lives long enough for us to figure this out. If he dies before we can, we'll have no choice but to do as our client directed and file the new will.

"Agree not to file and we share with you what we find. Then you can decide if you want a public fight or some accommodation.

"Don't agree — and Justin doesn't go. Don't agree — and he stays here helping prepare an argument for the Surrogate Court defending Jon's decision to give his entire estate to indigenous Africans as recompense for his part in hunting and murdering them.

"I can see the follow-up New York Post headline, 'New York Millionaire Hunted Africans for Sport: Family Fights to Keep Money from Victims.' It will have a photo of your father in a tuxedo and the rest of you at some big social event, printed alongside a picture of impoverished Bushmen. That'll be rough, I expect, for all of you, including the grandchildren."

Paul motioned to keep Gareth quiet and in his chair. "This is blackmail. How dare you threaten the family, the grandchildren."

"Stay focused on the facts and the law, Paul, and keep histrionics out of it. Our offer is good until tomorrow morning at ten."

Chapter 9

Msizi

Julia called Justin early the next morning. "Get a flight to Cape Town two days from now. Make sure you have your shots. You and Rogers interview Jon today. We need all the facts, $100 million worth."

She hung up.

Hours later, Jon, uncharacteristically, did not look up as Rogers shuffled into his room, Justin in tow. Covered in blankets, oxygen in his nose, the dying hunter stared despondently out the window to his left, as if seeing something troubling.

Rogers extended a hand that hovered unanswered above Jon's bed. "Nice to meet you, sir."

Jon did not turn his head. Rogers scraped a chair over to Jon's bed and sat heavily. Breaking the awkwardness of the moment, Justin sat in Jon's line of sight on the other side of the bed. Jon gave him a small smile.

"Since we first met," Justin told him, "I've done some homework on Bushmen. Your idea of a foundation is excellent, exciting. It could transform many Bushmen families, whole communities. We're all eager to make it happen."

Rogers abruptly interjected, his voice deep and somber, as if to balance against Justin's enthusiasm, "One or more of your heirs will challenge any change to the estate. The ensuing litigation might scuttle any idea of a foundation. That same litigation could result in loss of a substantial portion or the entire estate. We must move carefully to avoid that."

Jon's face darkened. Without turning to or acknowledging Rogers, he whispered hoarsely to Justin, "It's my money and I can do what I want with it."

"That's right," Rogers cut in, "but it's not that simple now. One of your children could convince a court that you're not mentally capable of making this last-minute change. Illness and medications have rendered you unfit to alter your will so substantially at this point. A court might conclude from your lifetime of business and philanthropic successes that your extraordinary claim from a hospice bed — that you hunted people for sport — is simply not believable."

"Happy to sign a confession," Jon snapped, still not looking at Rogers. *Why didn't you have the guts to say, "From your deathbed"?*

Justin sought to ease the tension, looking straight at Jon to get his attention. "Mr. Schmidt, my job is to take the information you give us today and use it to confirm your account of what happened. I'm flying to South Africa to find police reports, maybe some witnesses.".

Finally, somebody's on my side, thought Jon. *There may be something to this boy.*

As if hearing Jon's thoughts, Justin added, "For me, personally, helping you realize your vision for a foundation for Bushmen may be… will certainly be one of the most meaningful things I do in my career."

Jon gave him a weak thumb's up. Rogers shifted in his chair, causing it to creak, and reasserted himself. "Laudable as the goal may be, we must get there. So, start from the beginning, how you decided to go on the hunt in the first place."

Jon wheezed, hand over his nose, trying to bring in more oxygen. He nodded toward Justin.

"It started with the death of my closest friend, Msizi. His name means messiah in Zulu. Killed him. Makes me Pontius Pilate, I guess. He and I met while I was hunting in Natal. Justin, that's on the eastern side of South Africa."

Not in Kansas — not in Iowa any more, Justin thought.

"For years, we did every safari together. Rhinos. Lions. Leopards. Elephants. He liked to say that I covered the costs, and he covered my back."

Still speaking only to the young lawyer, he took almost a pleading tone. "Justin, son, you have to understand, I owed him my life." *Boy's going to need some proof.* "During the rainy season the first year we hunted together, we were headed out to an airstrip to pick up some clients. I was driving. We were stopped by a small breeding herd of elephants, no more than twenty, crossing the road. There were a few calves.

"Son, a 'breeding herd' is just what it sounds like. There are cows, bulls, calves. Ellies are much more protective than usual when calves are in the group. A young bull made a fake charge at us, but it was just that, bluster. We let the herd move on, calm down and get back to grazing.

"Got maybe fifty meters down the road when she attacked. A cow had left the herd and ambushed us. Hit us from Msizi's side of the truck. Knocked us right over. She backed up to decide what to do next. Msizi had fallen out, but I was caught by the steering wheel.

"I heard her coming back to roll the truck. Likely would have crushed me. Msizi ran a few paces back to get a better angle, twisted round and, while moving, put one right in her brain."

Jon studied Justin's face. He could see Justin's genuine interest, his focus. *Boy, you're getting the picture. Now hang on.*

"That's the friend Msizi was. Now, he was black, I'm white. We became like family in the 50s, just when apartheid was getting up to speed. That took some work, him being mistaken for a hired guide or porter, me putting up with racist shit from whites when I treated him like an equal. It made our friendship, to put it simply, unusual.

"He named his firstborn son for me, a white man. Unheard of in a traditional Zulu family. No one in his family was happy about it, except him and, well, me."

Rogers coughed as if to say, 'enough of the sentimental stories' and asked, "Mr. Schmidt, how does this Msizi's death relate to the Bushmen?"

Jon rolled onto his back and, for the first time, put eyes on Rogers. He sighed in visible disappointment with the obese lawyer and turned back to face Justin.

"When he was killed, I fell into my dark years. My mistake on that hunt killed him. It wrecked me. It's why I ended up years later with that murderous bastard."

Justin leaned forward, "What was Msizi like as a person? Help us know him, so we understand better what his death meant to you."

"Thank you, son. Appreciate you asking that," he said warmly. *Was right about you yesterday. For you, everything matters. Good lad.*

"Son, there was no better man in the bush in that part of Africa. Msizi was like most Zulu men, physically impressive. A head taller than me, a better shot, a better tracker. His rifle looked like a toy in his hands.

"Didn't finish primary school. But, you know, had a keen mind, loved poetry. One night I pulled Tennyson's *Charge of the Light Brigade* out of my pack. We did that back then, Justin. We read things other than iPhones, things called 'books.'" He winked. "Read that poem to him while he watched the flames at our feet.

"I knew it by heart as a child, like any good child of the British Empire. My mind is gone, can't remember it.

"Justin, you don't hunt except in libraries, maybe you know that poem?"

He had already pulled it up on his laptop. He knew what to do next, though Rogers was already huffing in impatience with the diversion.

Justin sat up and cleared his throat.

"Half a league, half a league,
Half a league onward,
All in the valley of Death
Rode the six hundred.
'Forward, the Light Brigade.
Charge for the guns,' he said.
Into the valley of Death
Rode the six hundred."

Hearing the verses, Jon's eyes flashed a deeper, younger blue. A smile pushed up his hollow cheeks, exposing long yellow teeth.

"Their courage — that's what Msizi loved about the poem. Msizi was convinced that all six hundred had Zulu fathers.

"Give us the last stanza, boy, the punch."

Justin scrolled down, and recited,

"Came through the jaws of Death,
Back from the mouth of hell,
All that was left of them,
Left of six hundred."

He looked at Jon. The old man's head was turned toward the ceiling, remains of white hair hanging off either side of his pink head. He raised a hand, motioning a 'thank you.'

His chest heaved. He was sobbing. With skeletal hands, he pulled the sheet up over his eyes.

Catching his breath, he lowered the sheet again and concluded, "Msizi could read only a few words of that poem. But once I had finished reciting it a second time, he stood by the fire and gave me all six stanzas of Tennyson's work — Tennyson with a Zulu accent.

"It was fitting that these verses were his favorites. Young men sent to early graves by someone's mistake. He was sent to his by mine."

"That day, the bull came straight at me, I had a shot. Not a chest shot — so I didn't take it.

"Bull circled around, came up behind Msizi. Opened him… opened him right up."

Jon turned his head to the window. Shaking fingers pinched his eyes as his chest rose and fell swiftly. Patrick offered him some water through a bent straw. Jon's shaking lips had trouble finding it.

"Left him out there. Had no choice.

"I went alone to his home. His family watched me slowly wind through their village without Msizi next to me. They knew what had happened. I heard his widow wailing when I got to his kraal.

"Jon, my namesake, on the hip of an auntie, taken away from me, away from the news of his father's death. Never saw him again."

Justin put a hand on Jon's bed, "I'm so sorry."

"It was my safari. The family knew that. I was responsible."

Rogers again interjected, too coolly, "Mr. Schmidt, how does this relate to you participating in a hunt of Bushmen?"

Jon frowned, groaned, and tried to sit up. Patrick adjusted the bed for him and pushed a pillow down his back.

"I'll explain the connection. But I need a break. We aren't into the worst of it, what his family did to me."

Chapter 10

Ubuntu

"If," Justin proffered over coffee in the cafeteria, "if Mr. Schmidt had a major breakdown because of the violence and shame of Msizi's death…" Here Justin came to the junction of human decency and legal strategy. "It could explain how a man, otherwise normal, might have done something so out of character."

"Long shot," replied Rogers with overt condescension. "Lose your perspective and you aren't doing your job. There is a line between being supportive and giving false hope. Back in the room, you were crossing that line."

About forty-five minutes later, Patrick called them back.

Jon hardly looked at the lawyers as they entered. He waited until Justin sat in his line of sight between the bed and window.

"Here's the descent, Justin," he began. "Here is where I turned to hating Black Africans, seeing them as *them*.

"Young man, I've never told anyone these stories. I'm counting on you to see this through."

"Yes, sir. I won't let you down."

Justin did not have to look up to feel Rogers's disapproval. He focused on Jon, who inhaled with impaired lungs and continued his story.

"Maybe two months after Msizi died, I got a letter from his father. Things were going badly. The baby no longer called 'Jon,' was sick. Msizi's widow was falling deep into a darkness that likely would take her. That deep depression can happen with Zulu widows.

"His father asked me to take him and his brother, Msizi's uncle, to the place where Msizi died. They would gather his spirit and bring it home to help heal the family. It's a Zulu belief.

"They hardly spoke for days as I led them to where it had happened. The place was a hell. Heat, animals, and insects had worked over his body and the carcass of the bull. I felt sick. I had seen death before. But this was my brother.

"They ignored the stench, the cloud of insects, Msizi's bones scattered around, torn clothing, the horror. They calmly opened grass mats and knelt. His father had brought a green buffalo thorn branch.

"Its thorns can capture spirits of deceased. They could take him home. His wife and son could recover.

"His father spoke to the small branch with soft words, whispering, calling Msizi's spirit to come with them.

"Stood there, that's all I did. Shameful. The mopane trees around me looked as dead as I felt.

"His father finished, rolled up his mat and left, alone. He carried the branch in front as he walked slowly down the trail. It now held Msizi's spirit among its thorns.

"The uncle stayed behind. He looked away from me when he finally spoke. I remember that because it was a sign of such disrespect.

"He raised both hands, 'How did this happen?'

"As I fumbled through an explanation — he only stared at the trail. He was tall like Msizi, powerful, deep black. He turned around several times, as if he could see the bull coming and his nephew being crushed and gored. Finally, he tilted his head down to look at me. 'You traded my nephew for a trophy?'

"No member of the family ever spoke to me again. I was shunned."

Justin looked up from his notes, brows raised in sympathy, "Shunned?"

"Zulus have a word, 'ubuntu' meaning 'a person is a person through other people.' If you banish someone, that man is no longer a person. He dies."

"They shun as ultimate punishment. It kills the human spirit."

Justin looked straight into Jon's eyes as he proceeded further into the story.

"Started serious drinking. Used opium sometimes. Anything to get numb. Went to shit."

Rogers, with a flat, antiseptic voice interjected, "I understand your pain. Where do the…"

Jon shot back sharply without turning his head. "Let me finish. I'm almost out of juice. You get this now or maybe never."

Rogers shifted his bulk.

Jon calmly addressed Justin. "Son, I grew up loving Africans. As a young hunter, I didn't give a care about race. I loved Msizi and his family. Truly."

Jon shook his hand in the air asking Patrick for water. Patrick held the cup as Jon drank from a bent straw.

He coughed.

"I thought maybe because of my love for them, in a racist country, maybe for that, they'd find a way to forgive me.

"But it didn't matter. As I've thought about it over the years, being white only added to the pain of their shunning. They rejected me, a white South African. A white man who accepted them, loved them.

"After that, drunk as I was, all Africans — whoever they were — were just that Zulu family that took my love and could show me no forgiveness. All Blacks became the people who rejected me. I learned to treat Africans with disrespect and anger, in amounts equal to my pain and the booze I lived on.

"You see? 'Ubuntu.' I stopped being a person.

"I had a flat in Durban. Hunted and guided a little. I wasn't good company. Clients didn't want a morose, drunk guide. Most of my time I spent in bars.

"Patrick, can you get me a little more?"

The African American hesitated.

Jon asked a second time, "Patrick, sorry, man, can I have some water?"

Their eyes met when Patrick brought the cup.

I see it in your face, thought Jon.

Patrick smiled and silently touched him on the shoulder while holding the straw to his lips.

Jon again felt the familiar knife edge of shame and averted his eyes from his nurse. Of the lawyers, he asked, "Ready for more? This is where hell starts."

Chapter 11

The Yugoslav

"Have to say," Jon acknowledged to Justin, "telling all this has lifted me a bit. Never told anyone what happened in those days, not my ex-wife, not my friends, not my children, not even my shrink. Shame's been so heavy."

Rogers, still ignored by Jon, tried to reassert himself, "Whatever detail you can provide, sir, it will help our defense."

Jon straightened and sat up a little.

"You get drunk enough, for long enough, and the lies become true. I told my drunk friends in the bar that Msizi was gored because he messed up. Failed to see the bull coming up from behind. That was his job, after all. He was backup. Convinced myself, at least on the outside, that it was his own mistake that killed him."

The impact of Jon lying about the death of his best friend, a death he had caused, took energy from the room. Justin stopped notetaking. Rogers just looked at Jon. Patrick did not move. Notwithstanding the sunlight, the room felt heavy, dark. Jon continued, recovering.

"Justin, you know how old I was when I took my first lion? Not a lion at rest, but one charging?"

"No, sir."

"I was thirteen. Rifle heavier than me." At first, it seemed another African hunting boast, causing Rogers to sigh. Jon ignored him. "You'll see how I got such a swollen head.

"My father and I were hunting after he got back from the war. There were lions about as we tracked a young giraffe cow. We came around some scrub and, in the middle of the track, just a few meters in front of us, was a juvenile male. I can see his short mane even now. He lay there in the middle of the trail panting at my father. His white canines, large tongue dripping.

"My father wasn't himself. In front of this lion, he just froze.

"I was behind him, so there was nothing I could do. Seemed like forever before he did anything. But it wasn't what I expected. He didn't raise his rifle, setting himself for the charge and a shot.

"He kept it down, resting in his left hand. He walked forward, toward the lion, talking softly, waving with his right hand, 'Go now. Go. I've nothing with you today. Go.'

"Predators don't like to be surprised. Lions, often, they're chickens. This young male was no exception. With a human walking up to him, he took off."

Jon coughed convulsively, putting his face into his pillow. Patrick had water ready when he recovered.

"Everyone out there knows that young males often travel in pairs.

"My father had forgotten or didn't care. He looked straight down the track where the lion had disappeared and kept walking, rifle tilted to the ground.

"I sensed it before I saw it, Justin.

"From the right, another male came at full throttle. Without time to think, I relied on routine, my dad's training. I shoved in a round, fell onto my right knee, counted, 'one, two.' I put a soft-nosed in his forehead."

By this time Justin knew Jon's stories had a purpose. He waited to hear how this one would help him on his trip to South Africa. Rogers noisily exhaled, as if wanting it to be over.

"Was telling that story to some drinking mates in Durban, back in my drunk days," Jon continued. "A guy at the end of the bar overheard it, laughed, waved me over, told me he wanted to hear more, offered me a pint. That's how I got to know Kuzman."

Rogers cut in, "So this is the man you were with in South West Africa?"

Of course, it is, thought Justin, gazing gently at Jon, to reassure him that, unlike Rogers, he was tracking the story and encourage him to go on.

"Good looking guy. Real charmer. Chatted me up about my safari work. Turned out we knew a lot of the same people. Had a few stories about mates we knew. He was a professional hunter, too. Guided when he could.

"Asked if I had any safaris going. Told him, no. It was slow." Jon looked straight at Justin.

"That's what he was waiting for."

The young lawyer was going to get what he needed.

"Kuzman said it was slow for him too, so he was heading northwest to help settler farmers. He said there were problems with Africans stealing and mutilating cattle. He was going to be part of a volunteer militia to protect the farms."

Justin thought of his memo, *In one all-nighter, he had nailed it. This actually happened.*

"Asked me if I wanted to go. Said first rate hunters like me were needed. I should've known he was all flattery and bullshit, but he was as smooth as I was stupid." There was lucidity, honesty, in Jon's eyes. "To be part of a militia — to protect white farmers against Blacks — seemed like a proper good idea."

He was dying in St. Lawrence of Manhattan. A last opportunity for truth.

"Looking back, I should've known better. There was never risk from Bushmen or Bantu like there was from the Mau Mau in Kenya. He used that lie to set the hook in my mouth, to get me to go."

Jon saw the lawyers sit up, always alert, sniffing for a defense. He brought them down.

"Let's be clear, I went willingly. I didn't have to go. I'm not bloody stupid. I was responsible for what I did and the deaths that followed. Get that down, Justin. Don't want any questions about that."

"Yes, sir."

"He said he would make arrangements. Knew people up there. Offered to pay my expenses, the train, truck hire, and all. Said he was thrilled to have my company. It was a lie, like so many he told me. He was broke. Once we were on the way, he hit me up for a loan to cover the trip. Said he'd pay me back with his first safari when we got back. He never made it back."

Justin leaned toward Jon. "He died on the trip?"

"Yeah. Killed by Bushmen. I'm getting to that.

"As we traveled to South West Africa, now called Namibia, he was non-stop chatting me up about my family, my hunts. He was good, got to say. Knew how to work me.

"As we neared the border, he boasted he'd be the best at protecting farmers. He was, in his words, 'a great hunter and patriot.' Told me how he left Yugoslavia after World War II when the Nazis lost. He fled to South Africa. He had to, he said. He and his partisan militia, according to him, 'had been too good at their job.' Spent most of his time, he said, hunting Gypsies and thieves, protecting his hardworking Slavic neighbors from *those people*.

"Jesus Christ. Right-wing partisans. Nazi supporters. I had heard from my father what they had done during the war. Nothing good about it. Here was one sitting in front of me.

"Like it was yesterday, I remember him leaning forward whispering over the train noise as if it was some grand secret, 'When the Germans surrendered, we went from being heroes to criminals. Protecting good people from thieving Gypsies was somehow a war crime.'"

Justin asked, "Did Nazi sympathizers find refuge in South Africa after the war?"

Before Jon could answer, Rogers interjected, pushing the conversation back to where it needed to be, "Mr. Schmidt, what did he say about Bushmen? Did he give an indication what he wanted to do?"

"It's been sixty years and I was drunk most of the time, but the gist of it was, 'Bushmen are half-man half-animal. They're dangerous pests. They kill cattle. They're thieves. Like Gypsies. But, unlike Gypsies, Bushmen can hunt, better than any white man.'"

Jon visibly shook at his memory of how Kuzman had taken the long list of Bushman qualities and twisted them. He shuddered at this own complicity, his silence at the time. "'They're criminals,' he told me. 'Dangerous. Live weeks without water. Follow tracks no matter how old. Arrows kill with a scratch. Best bush hunters in Africa. Can steal and kill cattle no problem. Farmers don't have a chance. Protecting against Bushmen takes skilled hunters like us.'

"Admit I was put off by the Gypsy and partisan stuff. Figured half or more was bullshit. Farmers needing help, on the other hand, made sense. I knew Bushmen could be dangerous.

"We were on our way. I had a bottle to keep me from getting sober and thinking clearly. In for a penny, in for a pound. Right?"

Rogers again interrupted, "Sorry, Mr. Schmidt, you have his full name, address, anything else on him?"

Jon motioned with his hand to make small hills in the air. "Figure his new permanent address is a few white mounds of hyena scat."

Turning back to Justin, Jon said sympathetically, "I see it in your face. You boy, you're thinking, 'we can justify this. Jon was just protecting farmers from cattle thieves on the frontier. Good for him, volunteering to be part of the militia. Whatever bad happened, the other maniac did it.' Right?"

Justin replied, "That's the line of argument I can see."

Rogers added, "Mr. Schmidt, that's also what it sounds like to me. If someone died while you were engaged in legitimate security work for farmers, we could change the will to pay damages. But leaving everything to unnamed Bushmen looks difficult with these facts."

Jon sighed with impatience. "There was nothing *legitimate* about what we did in Namibia. I'll explain if I have enough gas left."

His nurse raised the back of the bed. Jon inhaled deeply.

"Crossed over at Rietfontein. Lied to South African border control. Said we were game hunters. Drove to the farm of Mr. Van der Linden. Proper Boer farmer. Kuzman arranged for us to hunt from his place. Also told the farmer we were after big game. I paid the fee. That's where we started."

Sitting upright, increasingly more skeleton than man, he pressed against the back of his bed. "Let me finish this so you understand my responsibility for the deaths that came."

Saying that seemed to empty him. The remaining color drained from his face.

He rasped, "Tune in again tomorrow. Multiple counts of premeditated murder, true confessions, *The People vs. Jon Schmidt*."

Part III

Faded Desert Spoor

Chapter 12

Coke and Vodka

Justin's cell vibrated angrily at six a.m.

Julia. So early?

Her voice was clipped, emotionless. "Jon suffered a stroke last night. They're doing scans to figure out how bad it is. He's not conscious. You won't be able to get any more out of him. Change your flight and leave today."

"Sorry, what? That can't be."

"Justin, he can't communicate. He's comatose."

The young lawyer thought of Jon's humor and spirit of just the day before.

"He didn't finish the story. We could use more."

"We don't have time to see if he comes back from this. Rogers is pessimistic about our chances anyway. This stroke could take Jon out of the equation. We can't delay.

"Get to South Africa with the information you have. Start where he said they crossed into Namibia. Find witnesses and evidence."

Justin flashed on his abandoned Peace Corps plans. *This time it was happening for real.*

Julia added, "I don't have to tell you how much is riding on what you find over there," and hung up.

She next called Paul, who, in turn, informed his client.

"It was probably Julia's pressure," Paul told Gareth. "I hear her lawyers were over there interrogating him all day yesterday." He turned to strategy. "She called this morning to say she'd file if your dad dies before the young guy gets back from his little field trip. We know the filing would be a brutal account of what happened — of what your dad thinks happened. She'd likely send a copy to the New York Post just for the fun of it. I say we get ready with a response or a motion to seal, to put it under wraps — but hold off filing anything.

"We know what she's going to say. We'll outline how we'll respond and fill in details later. In the meantime, I'll have a psychiatrist visit your father to confirm he can't communicate and that the stroke was likely preceded by mini-strokes or significant mental impairment that led to delusions or confusion."

Gareth agreed. "We should wait. Don't want to be blindsided if they turn up a photo of dad holding a rifle over a dead Bushman."

Days later, on a highway that ran northwards from Cape Town, Justin was traveling to Rietfontein where he would begin his mission to corroborate Jon's story. To his right, the sun was flashing light over the Cederberg Mountains. Their jagged peaks seemed to invite adventure, to lure him into Africa. To his left, out of sight, was the Atlantic, the west coast of the African continent.

"All my American passengers love air-con," the driver told Justin as the minivan rumbled loudly. "My car reads thirty-two degrees outside, about ninety in American. I'll cool you off with my Japanese system. Reliable. Never fails."

Justin felt the van slow down as soon as the air was turned on. He smiled, settled back with his headphones, and moved to the left of the seat into shade. Jet lag overcame his excitement. He was asleep in minutes.

The next morning, far in the northwest corner of the country where it shares a border with Namibia, a heavy-set, very dark Border Security officer gestured to Justin to have a seat.

The border station was simple with faded green cement walls, the lower half showing years of grime. A photo of a serious-looking President Zuma hung awkwardly off center on the wall behind the officer's desk. In the center of the wall, in a larger, well-balanced frame, Nelson Mandela smiled warmly into the room. A secretary in a starched white blouse, her desk next to the officer's, stopped her staccato typing to gape at the young man.

The officer waved her back to work and leaned forward, as if to get a good look at this rare visitor. His sweat-marked uniform shirt, the color of the walls, strained at his bulk. Taking in Justin, he sat back, satisfied, his chair groaning.

"Welcome to Rietfontein. Never thought I would say that to an American lawyer or, frankly, any American who wasn't here on safari. Your driver said you wish to talk with us about an event in the 1950s. That's a new one."

"Yes, sir. I'm hoping to follow-up on some information from our client in New York."

"So, you are telling me this is serious?" Laughing, large white teeth filling his dark features.

Justin reflexively smiled in return. "Yes, sir."

"It might surprise you, young Mr. American lawyer, but I was not working here then. Was not born yet. And, whereas you are referring to a time long ago, we would need to consult our files. Being where we are, I am certain there are no files. But let me confirm."

Shouting to a colleague on the other side of the room, "Hey, Gabriel, were you here in the 50s? Files from then?"

"The 50s? No files. Was not alive. Doubt my father was. Hard to imagine who was here at that time." He seemed to dismiss the whole enterprise, but then added, "Maybe Seba. He might know something, if not drunk or dead."

"There you are Mr. Lawyer, all is not lost," grinned the border guard. "There is an ancient bugger, Sebastian, who might be of service. He is older than the sand, lives on the edge of town. He was working this border post in the 1950s, I'm sure. Wife died years ago. Has a San woman who cares for him. She lives at his place with her children. He must be in his 80s. People think she keeps him alive with Bushman potions. A true character if he's a little sober. More fun if he's not."

In front of the small house where Sebastian was said to live, Justin followed his driver through a gate made of irregular branches of dark wood that barely held strands of wire. A wire loop held it closed. Inside a fence, also of wire held haphazardly by oddly shaped posts, was plain dirt, light red. Goats stood bored in the heat. Two small children ran in circles trying to catch one of the chickens that clucked off as the children got close. The boy and girl, about the same age, barefoot in the dust, smiled and casually waved at the strangers.

The yard smelled of a trash fire. Ash rose from behind the house in clouds of dirty smoke.

Justin sniffed.

Who would have a fire in this heat?

The home was metal roofed with dark earthen-brick walls, punctuated only by two small windows on either side of a rough wooden door. To reach the door, both the driver and Justin had to bend under the edge of the roof's sharp corrugated metal.

A San woman, Sebastian's caregiver, opened the door before they knocked, a toddler attached to her with his arm tight around her leg. Justin and the toddler looked at each other, Justin smiling.

"Hello, young man."

The toddler silently chewed on a fist.

Justin turned his attention to the woman, the child's mother, for a little too long.

She's like a painting, beautiful.

His driver saved him, with a hand on his shoulder. "Ma, apologies for troubling you. This man is a lawyer from the United States, Mr. Justin. He is doing some important historical research and would appreciate a chat with Mr. Sebastian, if he might be available."

Justin recovered, turned his eyes to look behind the woman into the dark house as she stepped to the side.

"Pleasure. May you please come in. You can sit there. I am sure Sebastian will be happy to see you. Let me be right back."

The heat inside hit Justin like a wall. He arched his neck to look at the ceiling.

Metal roof. Damn.

He breathed deeply as he sat on a tired stuffed chair. He could feel springs under his thighs.

Wooden table and chairs, baby chair, small television powered by an extension cord hanging down the wall. Everything spotless. Children's toys neatly arranged. *I smell the kitchen from here. Something steaming, meat, vegetables, peppers. Bread baking.*

The toddler had stayed in the room when his mother left. He waddled over to the American and raised both hands in the air.

"He wants you to pick him up, Mr. Justin."

With the baby on his lap, Justin relaxed and took in more details of the house. The corrugated metal roof was exposed on its underside, broken by roughhewn rafters, all connected, it seemed, by scores of ominously large spider webs.

He's wet!

Handing the boy to his mother as she reentered, Justin glanced at the warm wet spot on his khakis.

"Seba's happy to see you. Oh, so sorry about your trousers. Nappies leak, you know."

"Thank you. It's not a problem."

"I'll get something to dry that spot."

Sebastian had propped himself up on pillows, several chins rolling beneath stubble and smile. With thin arms, he pushed himself up to sit taller, throwing his head back, displaying a solid Boer chin. Justin had some difficulty making out all his features, as Sebastian's face was in shadow with a window behind him. He could see, though, Sebastian's eyes and smile. Both expressed energy.

"So what can the oracle of Rietfontein do for you?" he began. "They tell you how long I've been here? I water-skied on prehistoric Lake Makgadikgadi when I first arrived. Only one who ever did."

"Sorry, sir. They didn't mention that."

"Unless you'd like to hear more lies, tell me what you need. Not much on my calendar. Plenty of time. Might be able to help."

Justin dug into his satchel, pulling out laptop and phone.

"Thank you, sir. I'm Justin McMann from the law firm of Cogswell & Worthy, in New York. Your colleagues at Border Security said you might know, if anyone would, about an event in the 1950s. Our client, now living in New York, hunted here as a young man.

There was apparently an incident that we are looking into. The death of a hunter."

Sebastian shook his head. "Got nothing with only that. Plenty died out there. Tell me a little more. A few more clues."

"Our client was a South African national. He was hunting across the border in Namibia, I guess it was called 'South West Africa' then. He was with a colleague, a man originally from Yugoslavia. He was also a South African, I think. Our client has told us that Bushmen killed his colleague. He managed to get to the border to report the matter and get help."

Sebastian looked over Justin's shoulder to the doorway and shouted, "Kanha, may you bring us some water or tea? Better be quick, this boy looks flushed. And a towel for his pants — and me a Coke with vodka. I'm going to need some juice. This boy just opened a book."

"Thank you," Justin said as the young mother put a glass of water on the table at his elbow and handed him an ironed, starched white towel. He only looked at the water.

Likely would kill me or give me something that would make me want to die.

Sebastian heard his thoughts.

"No worries, son. In this heat, you need to drink. Better than your New York water. Comes from a bore hole out back."

Bore hole? Justin chuckled at the comparison with the Central Park Reservoir.

He lifted the glass and tentatively took a sip, seemingly in exchange for a question, "Do you remember anything about this killing?"

Sebastian was mostly in profile due to the window light behind the bed. Justin heard loud gulps from the Coke can that Sebastian then set, with great ceremony, next to the vodka bottle.

"That killing was a major 'fok op,' as we say. This 'bru' who reported it, maybe he's your client. Some rich kid from Cape Town, wild story. I told him to stay in town for us to look into it. He didn't. Flew the coop."

Sebastian stretched for the vodka bottle, pouring some carefully into his Coke can that now had room for the liquor.

From outside the room, Kanha called, "Seba, you be easy on that vodka, or I will send the little one to sit on your bed."

"Of course, my love."

He held a finger to his lips while looking at Justin and pouring more liquor into the can, pushing himself with a satisfied sigh into his pillows.

"Are you like American lawyers in the movies? Gonna trap me with your questions and have me cry to the court, confess to the murder?"

He laughed at himself, coughed deeply, cleared his throat, and coughed some more. Kanha came to the bedroom door. He held up his hand and hoarsely said, "No, I'm OK.

"Lawyer boy, where do you want me to start?"

Justin's laptop illuminated his face in light blue, fingers already flying, seemingly on their own, noting details of the setting, date, time, Sebastian's house, Kanha; all facts to support the foundation of the interview.

"Sir, let's just walk through it sequentially — when the man came to you, what he reported, what happened next, what you did, what others did. But let's start with your full name, title at the time.

"And, my apologies, but do you mind if I make an audio recording? Some things just go too fast."

"Justin, I'll make you a deal. Have a good drink of that water, not a baby sip, just to prove you trust me, you believe what I am saying." Justin could only admire the technique. "Add to that, I don't want an American lawyer dying in my house from heatstroke. God knows what would happen then. Seal Team Six dropping down in my yard."

Face shining with sweat, Justin smiled and picked up the glass.

It can't be that bad. This guy's eighty. Nothing floating in it.

After seeing Justin take a drink and then another, feigning a smile and giving a thumbs up as he did, the old man exhaled, took a swallow of vodka-laced Coke, and dictated, "Sebastian Jansen. June 1, 1935. Two parents, mum, and dad, farmed on lousy land near Blyde River Canyon, other side of South Africa. Seemed we mostly harvested stones, tsetse flies and thorn bushes.

"Had to leave the farm, you know, find excitement, money. Signed up as a Border Security officer. Sent to Rietfontein after training. I was twenty. Won that bloody lottery, didn't I? Of all the places. There was less here then than now, not that it matters much because, hell, it's been mostly a good time."

"Sorry to interrupt, but for my notes, can you give your address and phone number?"

"You see a street sign on the road? Or a number hanging on one of my goats? No, just mail me in Rietfontein. Everyone knows me. Don't have a phone. No one to call. My sweetheart can hear me without one."

He lifted the vodka bottle and set it back loudly.

Kahna shouted, "Seba, I can hear that."

Sebastian whispered conspiratorially, "See? Small house."

Discreetly lifting the bottle off his bedside table with his eyes on the bedroom door, he said softly, "Want some vodka in your water? Might make the story more interesting and kill the bugs in it."

"No, thank you, sir."

"Kidding, of course. Vodka won't kill those bugs."

Is he joking or am I going to die?

"Lawyer boy, where was I? Right, I'm alone at my post when this truck with South African plates comes from the west, moving all too fast, bouncing, kicking up lots of dust. Rude to do that so close to the post.

"Young guy gets out, alone, filthy, whole body covered with bush dirt, head to toe, breathing hard. He had what we called the 'smuggler's look,' eyes jumping around.

"Too fast, too fast, I remember, he starts telling me about hunting with a partner when Bushmen attacked, apparently for no reason, lobbing arrows at this guy and his friend. If you know Bushmen like I do, you know that story is bullshit. If you do any sort of police work, you also know that when someone rapid-fire volunteers you a story, it's also probably bullshit.

"But I listened, looked at his *Persoonskaart*, his identity card, and that of his partner. He hands me his friend's card; says he was buried out there somewhere. Guy didn't know where.

"Don't remember their names. Wrote them down and their card numbers. Don't know where that paper might be. No files around here, you know.

"So, this is all I have, what I have up here," tapping his head.

"This is good, sir. Very helpful."

"You have some more water while I get some of this nutritious Coke in me and we'll continue."

On the table next to where he placed his glass, was a small, framed photo of a broad-shouldered man with a square jaw and large smile, an arm around a woman who looked straight at the lens without smiling, seemingly annoyed at the picture-taking or the man holding her.

"Is this a picture of you and your wife? You in uniform?"

Sebastian downed some Coke-vodka, burped, and sighed. "That beauty was my Katherine. Didn't deserve her. She shouldn't have had to serve here with me, but she was a strong one. Never complained. She grew up on a rock farm, like me. Lost her eighteen years ago."

"You look pretty good in that uniform. Would you mind if I took a picture of this with my phone?"

"Go ahead. Want royalties if I see it on a movie poster. Look over on that wall. Katherine had my badge framed with my certificate of service. You might want a picture of that as well if you are going to prove you really spoke with this ancient prophet.'"

As Justin took the photos, Sebastian said, "Let me fix this Coke with another milliliter of vodka, per Kahna's prescription, and get back to my tale — or his tale, which was a tall one.

"This bloke was either a moron or a killer because, what he said anyway, was that he and his mate were, just the two of them, hunting kudu or other big game out where they'd never been before. Now, I might've done so brilliantly on my exams that I earned a posting here but I'm not stupid. Two white guys from South Africa, hunting large game in new territory, no guide, no porter? Something's up with him is what I thought. Seemed to me he set out to murder his partner. That made more sense. He confirmed it for me.

"Gave me a line about an ambush by murderous, thieving Bushmen. Like they're pirates or something.

"It gets worse. Bugger had no money, empty pockets. Nothing. Incredibly, wait for this gem, except for those two ID cards. Bloody hell. He said he had put his and his mate's ID cards in his pants pocket just before the ambush. Said he barely escaped the attack to get to old man Van der Linden's place." Sebastian paused." You're the lawyer. Make sense to you?"

"No, sir."

"I know that farmer, Van der Linden, or knew him. Dead now, good bloke. That's where your client said he had left his truck and retrieved it after escaping the Bushmen. Something was very fishy here. Van der Linden would've helped him. Would've given him supplies, water, a firearm. Van der Linden also would have immediately notified authorities of the Bushman attack.

"Story was nonsense. But he said it happened; he said his partner, a white guy, got killed, ambushed by San inside the Police Zone. That bit of news was a big deal then, would be still. We had a lot of questions for this guy."

"Sebastian, sorry to interrupt, but did the identity cards back then have photos on them?"

"Yes."

Handing over his laptop, Justin asked, "Can I show you these pictures of our client? This is him in the mid-1950s. Does he look familiar?"

Sebastian took the laptop, the screen illuminating a heavy face lightened by mischievous eyes. "Can't say he does. Only been sixty years, for Chrissake. He looks like about a thousand white guys from back then."

Justin sat back down, and Sebastian continued, "Anyway, get this into your report. I put the guy into a room at a boarding house. He promised to pay when his father sent money. He also gave me his word he would stay in town while we investigated this mess. Asked me for some money and if there was a bar nearby. I said 'no' to both.

"Way I saw it, this 'domkop' probably murdered his partner. The story about bloodthirsty Bushmen was just that, a story. How did he escape from these 'murdering Bushmen' without a weapon? No one, no one, is better at tracking than them. They would have found him and finished the job. He would've been 'done and dusted' in a hundred meters.

"Why travel to the border to report to us in South Africa if he was attacked in South West Africa? You know that was a different country, right? That's why we had a border post. Border and all that."

"Yes, sir, I understand."

"So, he makes it out of the bush by some miracle, recovers his truck, doesn't stop to get help or anything and makes a bee-line for South Africa.

"Thinking about all this now, with a little help from this nutritious beverage, I remember something unusual he kept repeating. He said, 'I just couldn't do it.' That was odd when I heard it then and it's still odd now. I asked him 'what couldn't you do?' He would only say, 'Just couldn't.'

"I didn't want to be alone in this cock-up, a likely murder inquest. Didn't have authority for that sort of thing. I'd just had the bad luck of being on duty when he drove up."

Justin wiped his forehead. "Sorry, why couldn't you and your office handle the matter? He was a South African, right? You were police here, right?"

"My office controlled the border, not murders in the bush on the other side of the border. I notified mates in the South West Africa military. If a murder happened, it happened on their turf. If rogue Bushmen had done it, they needed to find out fast and take care of it.

"I also wanted them to come and question him. It was their crime file, not mine. They never had a chance. Seemed like the day after he got here, Cape Town boy left town. His daddy sent a lawyer in a Land Cruiser. I remember. Nice bush vehicle. Just came out. Discussions were had with my supervisors. Promises made that he would be available for the inquest. The lawyer escorted the guy out of town.

"Think about that. Likely murderer. Guy leaves town, following his lawyer down the road. Never knew what happened to him.

"I do know what happened here, though. South West Africa soldiers took some San trackers and headed to Van der Linden's farm.

"Rich boy had said he didn't know where the body was. Bloody idiot. Troops followed his bootprints from

Van der Linden's place back into the bush to the exact spot where it had happened.

"You know they found the body and weapons, right?"

Justin shook his head 'no,' and lifted his phone to be sure it was still recording.

"Yeah, they found it several days' walk northwest from the farm. Every step he had taken was obvious to the San trackers. Want some vodka yet?"

"No, thanks."

"Tell me if you do. That water might be getting to you."

Chuckling, he continued, "The body, what was left, hyena had worked it over. Given its condition, they couldn't tell what had killed the man. Pieces missing, chewed up pretty good, you know.

"One of the trackers was an older Bushman. Dear mate of mine. He and I, well, mostly him, we had found our share of smugglers together. This old man, Xau, he could find tracks at night in a windstorm, he was that good. I heard that, while others were focused where the body parts were, he circled away, examining, as a good tracker would, everything."

Justin expected from what Jon had told him that a careful inspection by a Bushman was going to reveal just about the whole story.

"He found Bushman prints. He said it looked as if one San had come to the area where the body was and then left. Might've just been someone who stumbled onto the mess. Hard to say.

"Xau followed the prints.

"You had to know this guy. Maybe four-and-a-half-feet tall. When I worked with him, I would tease him, 'Xau, you always find prints because you have to climb over them to go anywhere.' He *loved* me. I miss him. He's dead. Years ago. My Kahna, she's his granddaughter. We're family."

Reminds me of Jon's relationship with Msizi, thought Justin.

"You know what the tracker found?"

"Another body?"

"No, man! What's in that water? Another body? That's crazy.

"They found two packs and two pricey rifles with scopes. All buried in the dirt. Can't even guess what happened. No one abandons their gear out there — buries it even — unless they're mad. Walking the bush with no firearm? Suicide.

"My mates across the border brought all that to us, the packs, rifles. Something had gotten into the packs, torn them up a bit, but they were intact.

"Clothes, first aid supplies, small telescope for game spotting, about ten rounds in each pack. Usual stuff. Remember one had letters in it from Yugoslavia. Noticed the stamps. Had never seen any from there before.

"Rifles were first rate, H&H .375 mags, standard for big game. Nice scopes. Even with the sand in them, we could tell only one had been fired and that one, only once. Had four rounds left in its magazine. The other had a round sitting in the chamber and four in reserve. That one hadn't been shot.

"I had thought from the start that the Cape Colony boy had killed his partner and this sort of proved it. Thanks to the hyenas, no one could say how the bugger died, whether he was shot or what. The remains, the pieces they could gather, they took to Windhoek. Didn't see them."

Justin had a pain in the pit of his stomach. *This is not what Jon described.* "What do you think happened out there?"

"I think that Cape Towner killed his partner, panicked, came up with a story of Bushmen attacking them. Throwing all the gear and rifles away was a clumsy way of supporting his story. Or he just went mad. That happens out there. Either way, he was guilty.

"I heard he soon left South Africa for America. Not something an innocent victim would do now, is it?

"Sad to say, the local San bore the brunt of it. After his lie about the Bushman attack got out…" he began coughing uncontrollably.

Kanha came to the room. She smiled sweetly at Sebastian as she stroked his hair and propped him up. She had him sip some tea and rubbed his chest. After a few minutes, he recovered.

"Sorry, young man. You're looking like you feel worse than me. Are you OK?"

"Might be the heat. The story, him murdering his partner; it's troubling."

"Well, sorry. Life out here is that way, a trifle troubling."

He coughed again. "I think this is it for me. Told you what I know. Feeling like a rest."

"Thank you for everything. Before I go, do you think it would be worth a trip to Van der Linden's farm to see if anyone there remembers any of this?"

"Never hurts, you know, talking with more people. Solid police work and all that. And you'll see a bit of Namibia. Have your driver ask around for directions." Sebastian sighed with fatigue. "And if you want more that is close by, I recommend you go to the combined school. Ask for Mr. Williamson. He teaches there. His father was a journalist back then. Wrote about the murder and what happened to the Bushmen. Williamson might have saved his father's articles."

Kahna walked Justin and his driver to the gate.

"I know Seba enjoyed talking with you."

Turning back before getting into the minivan, Justin saw Kahna politely waiting at the gate to see them off, smiling, waving with one hand, the toddler on her other hip. With a foot, she blocked a chicken from escaping. She closed the gate, returning to the house and her Seba.

Chapter 13

Namibia

Back at the guest house where he had Wi-Fi, Justin sent an email,

Julia,

I had a productive day in Rietfontein.
I located a retired border guard who recalled with clarity some of the events our client reported, such as date, place, and general circumstances. I have a detailed interview that I recorded.

Somewhat problematic is that he and other officials believed at the time that our client killed his hunting companion. Their assessment does not support our client's account of the events.

I am traveling into Namibia tomorrow to the farm where the hunt began. There might be witnesses there. I also have a lead on some newspaper articles that I am tracking down.

Best regards,
JS

Julia responded within minutes,

> *Call me when you return from Namibia. Don't*
> *email.*

> *Julia*

The next day, Jason peered over his shoulder to look into the swirl of dust trailing the minivan. The border post had faded out of sight. Namibia looked exactly like South Africa as far as Justin was concerned. Sparse vegetation marked sandy hills. He could see cattle and farm buildings from time to time. The further they went, the rougher the road became. He was jostled side to side or up against the car roof, depending on the moment.

"Don't worry, Mr. Justin, my vehicle is strong and knows these dancing roads of Africa. I will stay in the middle track where it is smooth."

Within minutes, he heard the woeful 'flap, flap' of an injured front tire. Dust settled over them as the driver got out to inspect. Justin stretched his back and surveyed where they were. Sand and scrub were about all he saw. Some distance away on a small hill, he could make out the profile of a boy standing near some cattle. He waved. The boy waved back.

"Mr. Justin, this will be done right fast, no worry. Don't wander from the vehicle. We don't know what's there. Might be snakes, you know."

Justin walked several paces down the road, inspecting the soft sand on the sides. *Is that a snake track? No clue.*

The driver called him back as he was proudly putting the flat tire into the back of the van. He had barely said, "All done, see?" when he noticed a back tire had also deflated. Justin kicked it and looked at the driver.

"I don't imagine you have a second spare."

The driver's phone did not have a signal. They opened the doors and windows of the van and settled in. The wind was hot as it passed through the vehicle.

"This is Africa, Mr. Justin. Someone is always nearby. You will see."

Justin looked again at the hill, shimmering now in the heat. The boy was gone.

Morning turned to afternoon. Justin and the driver shifted in the vehicle to stay in the shade. The wind got hotter and stronger. Justin shaded his eyes to see up and down the road. *Nothing. Wonder if we'll die out here?*

When the sun set, the temperature quickly fell. They went from uncomfortably hot to cold, confirming for Justin that he was going die, now from cold. They closed the van doors and windows. The driver began running the engine and heater for a few minutes at a time. Justin kept vigil looking behind them through the driver's dust-covered side mirrors. Eventually, a pair of headlights appeared.

His driver got out and approached what Justin could see was a dark green, dust-covered Land Cruiser. To Justin, it looked like a proper safari truck. It rode high with a stout front grill and winch. Its driver had not descended, having only rested an elbow out of his open window. Justin overheard him say, "Odd place for a South African taxi. You get lost?"

"No, sir," replied the driver. "Mr. Justin is an important American lawyer on his way to the Van der Linden farm. He is engaged in some historical research."

"Well, you are on the road that leads to the farm. Headed there myself. Throw in your two flats and maybe that important American lawyer and I can take all three to Van der Linden's place. Probably best you stay with your vehicle, or you might lose your remaining wheels before we get back."

An hour later — long enough for Justin to answer questions about his research — a few big dogs greeted the Land Cruiser as it pulled up to a modest white farmhouse. A heavy-set African woman looked up from a garden alongside. "Welcome home, Mr. Jacob."

Jacob brushed the dogs back. "Boys, you stay out. You've never smelled an American lawyer, but that's no reason to be rude."

The interior of the house was dark and cool. A small fire burned in a fireplace between windows. Facing the fire was a high-backed chair, with an ottoman. A thin, white-haired woman turned her head toward the door when the men entered. Noticing Justin, she self-consciously straightened the blanket on her legs with weak hands and modestly placed her feet on the floor.

"Mother, meet Justin. He has come from America with questions about those South Africans who hunted from here when the one was killed.

"He says the other is still alive in America and has sent him to make a report on what happened. This is not about us or the farm. It's about that man wanting to change his will or something. I told him what I recall, but I was a little lad at the time. You'll have a sharper memory."

The woman eyed Justin wordlessly. She faintly smiled at Jacob who said, "Justin, have a seat. You two can chat while I fix the tires." Seeing that his mother remained suspicious and silent, he added, "Mother, it's fine, you can talk to him. It might help some Bushmen here. I told him he could record your conversation." She responded by smoothing her hair, worn in a tight bun.

"Mrs. Van der Linden, my client has asked me to help confirm what happened. I understand the military came and found his colleague's body and their equipment."

She cleared her throat. Her voice was stronger and deeper than Justin anticipated. He checked that his phone was recording.

"It was long ago but it produced quite a racket here where we live quietly. Very disturbing what happened. My children were young at the time, too young to hear about murder and death."

"I'm sorry to make you think of this again. Any information you can give me will be helpful."

"I remember it clearly, the way a mother remembers a danger to her children. Those men sat at my table with my family. They had come to hunt. That is what they told my Carl. They lied. Instead, they brought violence to our farm.

"One was polite, the small one, the one from South Africa. The other, the one who died, I did not like him from the start. He was smooth, like we say. Someone not to be trusted. He talked a lot. Had an accent from Eastern Europe, a foreigner.

"This man insulted my family and the Africans who live on our farm and are our friends. He asked about Bushmen. He said he had heard they were dangerous to us and other farmers. He asked Carl if they caused us problems." She paused, then spelled out the next phrase slowly. "He said he could help by *clearing — them — off* our land."

It was distasteful for her to say it.

"That was too much for my Carl and me. 'Dinner's over,' said Carl. I took the children from the kitchen. He took the men outside and had them sleep in the barn.

"Understand, we had no problem with Bushmen. Many worked for us. They are children of God, as are we."

"What did the smaller man say, the South African?"

"When they were outside, I heard him angrily arguing with the foreigner. They clearly didn't like each other. The larger man bullied the smaller one. I believe, as did Carl, that this explains the murder."

"Before we get to that, do you mind if I show you some photos?"

She sat up straighter as Justin knelt by her chair holding his laptop open to pictures of Jon in his twenties.

"That's him, the smaller one, the polite man, the murderer. He's your client?"

Justin nodded and considered how to challenge her conclusion without losing her trust. "Ma'am, I have an important question. What makes you think he murdered the other man?"

"The South African, your client, came back alone from the hunt. He had no game, no rifle, nothing. Carl saw him walk to his truck. Carl said he was weak and staggered more than walked as if the desert had almost killed him.

"Carl offered him food and water, asked him about the other man, did he need help? Your client only drove away. He said nothing. That is not something an innocent man does.

"Days later, the soldiers came. Let me show you a picture." Pointing to a wall, she said, "Hand me the large one in the middle, with the trucks and men. I never liked that photo, but Carl did. So, I keep it up where he had it."

Justin took down a framed black and white photo, scarred by a few creases, but clear. There was a line of men, shoulder to shoulder, standing stiffly. Five were in military uniforms. One civilian stood between them, and three Bushmen stood apart on the right. Behind them were two army trucks. Cursive handwriting in black ink along the white margin read 'August 18, 1955.'

"This is my Carl," she said pointing to the white man in civilian clothes. "These soldiers had come to search for the man your client killed. With these Bushmen trackers, they found the body and their packs and guns." Tapping the photo, "On the back of this truck was a box that had that man's remains. They said animals had eaten most of him. I think it was God's punishment."

Justin needed somehow to get her to acknowledge an alternative version of events. "Could it be instead, ma'am," he began, but the contradiction was too stark. He thought harder. "Ma'am, you said the dead man had made disparaging comments about Bushmen at the table. Shockingly so."

This she readily confirmed. Justin was on his way.

"Could it be, ma'am," he offered gently, "is it possible he went out to the desert to harm them?"

If she did not endorse this theory, at least she might not reject it. He continued, "And that, in self-defense, the Bushmen killed him?"

"Young man, I have lived here all my life. Bushmen are gentle people. But if they are threatened and need to strike back, they will." Her expression was set firm. "If Bushmen had been responsible, your client would have met the same fate as his partner. Instead, he just walked out of the desert, with no weapon."

She read Justin's face. He was crestfallen. But she knew the San. "If Bushmen had hunted him," she repeated, "he, too, would have been brought out in a box."

Justin asked if he could take a photo of the 1955 picture. He hung it back on the wall and walked toward the door.

"Thank you, again."

"I can see this is not the news you wanted. Africa isn't like that, I'm afraid, you can't just arrange everything the way you want it, like New York, on a grid of numbered streets." She set kind eyes on him. "I will pray for you and ask God to forgive your client."

Turning at the door, Justin made a last try. "Those Bushmen in the photo, are any of them still around?"

"No. Xau, the oldest and smallest of the three died years ago. He is the one next to Carl. They were friends. The other two went north into Botswana. That's where many Bushmen from here moved. I understand many now live near Ghanzi."

Chapter 14

Dispatch

Late that evening at a guest cottage, Justin pulled open heavy red curtains. They revealed a grey cinderblock wall behind the room's one small window. The wall was a hand's breadth away, the space between window and wall too tight to let anything pass. The cinderblocks were unpainted, topped by broken bits of different colored glass. The red, green, and white glass shards were brilliant under security lights.

Super-max prison? That wall is maybe four inches away. What are they expecting to get in here?

He pulled closed the window, wrestling the rusted latch to catch, sealing the window shut. He closed the curtains so that one pleat covered another. No light or air could get in. The room's temperature immediately increased.

His driver was down the hall, quite pleased that the cottages had a pool after his tire-induced stress in Namibia. He would not be around to hear any of Justin's call home.

The one fan in the room ran rough, wobbling on its axis, threatening to come loose at any minute.

"Julia, I hope this is a good time."

"Justin, yes. How are things going?"

"Made some good progress."

"I'm conferencing in Rogers."

Justin reported how he had been able to confirm key elements of Jon's account, including place, date, and general circumstances. He relayed how he traveled into Namibia to speak with Mrs. Van der Linden who, also, had a sharp recollection of the events. He described the photo of the military on the farm.

"In addition to these interviews, I got copies of articles from a local Gazette. The journalist is now deceased but his son, a schoolteacher, had a binder of his father's articles. They provide the date of reported death of Kuzman, his full name and that of Jon. The articles corroborate elements of events Jon reported to us, such as his flight from South West Africa and the story he told the border guard. And pretty much confirm what the retired guard and Mrs. Van der Linden told me."

Time to show them I've been thorough, he thought. "I'm reading from the North Cape Colony Gazette,

Rietfontein, South Africa, August 15, 1955, Douglas Williamson for the Gazette.
Reported, Bushmen Attack*. Mr. Jon Schmidt of Cape Town informed authorities in Rietfontein on August 12 that a band of San men assaulted him and his*

hunting companion, Mr. Kuzman Horvat, also of South Africa. Mr. Horvat died in the attack. Mr. Schmidt escaped through the desert and made it to the border to report the crime. Authorities are investigating.'

"Good work," hummed Julia. "Third-party sources are always persuasive. Before we go further, your room is isolated, right?"

"Yes," Justin reassured her. "Now here's where we have a problem. The border guard and the farmer's wife are of the view that Jon killed Kuzman. The guard thinks the whole story about the Bushmen was Jon panicking. The widow stresses that Jon couldn't have escaped the desert if Bushmen had been hunting him.

"Forensics doesn't help us. Both told me animals had badly mutilated the body. Hyenas, apparently. Enough parts were missing that authorities couldn't tell what killed him. That means that, as of right now, everything I've found points to Jon shooting Kuzman. The widow said the two argued bitterly while at the farm and that Kuzman was pushing Jon around.

"I have found nothing to date," it hurt him to admit, "that supports Jon's claim that Bushmen killed Kuzman when the two of them stalked the Africans."

I haven't yet helped Jon or the Bushmen, he thought. To hide his disappointment, he ticked off in a staccato fashion his other findings — the ID cards, buried gear, the rifle fired only once.

His voice expressing disappointment, he slowed, "Little of this jibes with what Jon told us or what he told the border official about being ambushed by San. Nothing I have found so far suggests Jon was on a militia mission that went bad. There are too many inconsistencies. He may well be confused about all of this." He hated to say it. He pressed on, unable to let it stand at that: "It just doesn't add up. We're missing a lot, important pieces."

"No," Rogers interjected and seemed to dismiss Justin altogether, "Julia, I think we have all the pieces we need. We're done. From the beginning, this was an improbable tale told by a dying man. Against that improbability is the weight of $100 million. We move forward with this and we, the firm, lose. As it stands now, we're likely going to eat the cost of Justin's safari trip, this junior Raiders of the Lost Ark adventure."

Julia ignored Rogers. "Justin, I can't get my head around Jon killing his hunting partner and making all this up. Could these people have it wrong? They are all pretty old by now, at least as old as Jon. None actually saw what happened."

"Right and the guard drinks a lot. But he had a vivid memory of Jon, what he said and did. It lined up with the widow's memory. And there are more news articles, one that helps." He paused to create anticipation, to add emphasis.

"A follow-up story reported that a volunteer militia group set out to hunt down the Bushmen Jon said had attacked them. The militia combed the area, found two

Bushmen, and lynched them. They burned huts of several Bushmen families and forced them out of the area." He was feeling strong again. "Objective third-party source, Julia, and it's consistent with what Jon told us about these militia."

He paused for a reply or question. The phone was silent.

A long moment passed before Rogers huffed, "Julia, end it here. Kill this. An allegation that Jon killed Kuzman would be fatal to Jon's request to change his will. Once the other side learns this, they'll use it to prove he's delusional and his whole Bushman story is horseshit. They'll sue us. Remember, you promised them we would share what Justin found."

Justin could hear her exasperation. "OK, OK, Rogers," she spit out. "I got it. Justin, send us what you have and come back."

"I might be able to find Bushmen who remember something." He said it so naturally that it seemed normal until he heard the silence it prompted. But he was immersed in his hunt — he was adapting to his environment and gaining confidence. "When I spoke to the schoolteacher, he said that the San themselves might be the best source of information about what happened out in the bush near here, even back in the 1950s. He told me that Bushmen have a strong tradition of recounting their history through stories passed from one generation to another.

"I asked him if he had an idea where the Bushmen from this region went after the militia lynched those two men and destroyed settlements. He said many relocated to Ghanzi, Botswana, where Bushmen have settled over the years. The widow repeated the same thing. I think I can…"

Rogers interrupted, "Horseshit on horseshit. You're telling us you want to go on another safari to maybe find *some* Bushmen who *maybe* heard a story around the fire — a story that we are supposed to use to convince a New York judge that some fantasy about hunting humans is real? I didn't know delusion was contagious. Julia, I'm done. This is unethical." He hung up.

Justin tilted his head back and silently screamed at the ceiling of his room. *Listen to me!*

He waited.

"Justin, I appreciate your determination and good work," she said. "But we can't keep chasing ghosts. Come home." It sounded hollow, so she added, "End it."

With as impassive a voice as he could manage, Justin replied, "Understood."

Chapter 15

Ghanzi

"Mr. Justin, wake up, please. We are almost there."

Justin sat up, arching his back, stretching his neck and shoulders.

Damn. Twelve hours in this van. This guy drives ten miles an hour. Seems to aim for potholes. It's already getting dark. Most dangerous time on African roads. Animals colliding with cars. Where are the zebras and elephants? Probably waiting to cross in front of us.

Through the van's panoramic sloping windshield, he caught a large sign, faded by the sun, advertising "Grasslands Bushman Lodge" with an arrow pointing to the right, into what seemed to be nothing but scrub and sand.

African irony? Haven't seen grass in days.

Turning left off the two-lane road, bumping off irregular asphalt to even more irregular dirt, the driver slowed, turned, and said, "Here we are, sir. Ghanzi. Would you like straightaway to find our hotel and a bite to eat? Might be a good idea, given the hour."

"Yes, thank you. We can look for some contacts tomorrow." *Hotel. This is going to be on my nickel, I expect, now that I'm AWOL. Firm won't cover my expenses, that is, if I even have a job when I get back.*

Ignoring Julia, he had acted on both instinct and training, reading the tracks he had found, refusing to leave the hunt. Once he made his decision to continue, he felt a freedom, a lightening of his spirit that he had not felt since before his father died. He was on his own. He could make a difference.

Jon filled his thoughts. *His eyes were not lying. He was clear in what he said. There's no way he is making this up.*

The next morning, waking in Ghanzi, he checked his phone. Nothing. *They think I'm on the way home.* He folded himself once again into the back of the dust-covered van and unzipped his satchel to double-check the battery charge on his phone and laptop.

Without looking up, he asked the driver, "Did you understand from the clerk where we go to find Bushmen?"

"Yes, sir. Right where we got off the road. Their homes are all along there, close to town."

It took five minutes.

They fell in with trucks that kept up their speed and barely moved to accommodate people walking on either side of the dirt roadway. The van driver cut right just before the dirt road transitioned to pavement. He drove onto a soft sand road that curved easily through a maze of fences made of odd-sized sticks and wire. The houses seemed haphazardly arranged with sand passageways between them, marking irregular small lots. This was a place where many Bushmen families lived.

Justin dictated into his phone, "On either side of us are what look to be one-room dwellings with corrugated metal roofs sloping off to one side. Each one has children, chickens, and other small livestock in front. Young men are gathered at the intersection where we turned."

A minivan with South African plates and a white man inside had the same effect it would have in any African small town: curiosity and welcome.

Justin slid open the side door, checking reflexively that his satchel was safely within the vehicle, and stepped out to greet the half dozen young men standing near the van.

"Good morning. How are you gentlemen?"

One, apparently the oldest, in a clean white tee shirt, long pants, and sandals, jostled with his friends and stepped forward, flashing a broad smile.

Extending his hand, he said, "Good morning, sir. Your vehicle is South African, but you do not sound South African. Are you British?"

"No. American."

"Pleasure to meet you."

Justin shook his hand and everyone else's. In short order, small children ran up, barefoot, dusty, smiling. He knelt to shake with exaggerated ceremony their hands as well.

Standing, with the youngest children pushing to be closest to him, Justin dusted off his pant leg and turned to the boy in the white tee shirt.

Before Justin could speak, the young man asked, "Are you looking for a game drive? Maybe Bushman art?"

"No. I'm doing historical research." Eyes widened all round him. "Looking for San or their families who perhaps sixty years ago may have come from much further south, near the northwest corner of South Africa, close to Rietfontein. Or just west of there over the border in Namibia. I understand that many moved from there to here."

The young man ran his hand back and forth over his short hair. "Sir, excuse me, I do not know that town. But there are some old people here who came from the south. The oldest man I know lives over there," pointing toward the end of the settlement. "If you want, I could inquire for you. He is home all the time now, he is so old."

Moments later, emerging from the dwelling of the old Bushman, the young man waved Justin over. The lawyer lifted his satchel onto a shoulder and reached across the minivan seat for two bottles of honey.

The hotel clerk said this would be a good gift.

As he walked toward the house, the other young men stayed near the van chatting with the driver. Small children trailed Justin, dancing around him and chirping questions or a few English words until one of the women at the door of a hut shouted at them. They scattered.

The boy said, "This way, please."

Justin took in the small courtyard.

They swept the dirt. Two short stones set together in the sand with something painted on them. Like Egyptian symbols.

Another metal roof! Hoping for fewer spiders.

Approaching the doorway, dark under the shade of its slanted roof, he avoided water stains in the sand and dodged buckets, one of which contained soapy water. The pails looked like they had been abandoned moments before. Clothes waved in the wind, suspended on a wire running from the house to the fence.

Above the rippled metal roof, the sky was a deep blue, cloudless. A hint of a new moon rose over trees on the other side of the road.

Before entering, the American paused.

Someone's walking to the door, shuffling. Stick hitting packed sand.

As soon as this man stepped into the morning sunlight, Justin felt his cheerfulness. It seemed to radiate through the doorway. Deep wrinkles around his eyes matched those over his whole body. He wore only a leather brief. He appeared frail as though there was no substance behind the dark brown skin that draped over his small frame.

He was barely taller than a child, at most four foot six. But it was hard to tell how tall he was since he stooped forward at the waist. He appeared to keep from folding over completely with the help of a smooth, elegantly carved stick. He held it lightly in his left hand.

Given his appearance, Justin expected a weak handshake. But the man's grip was firm, his fingers strong, calloused. The Bushman's hand conveyed the energy his face exuded. He simultaneously shook Justin's hand, greeted him in Bushman, lowered his head and reached for the young man's satchel. While he did all that, he lifted his walking stick as if it were nothing.

Justin raised a hand, signaling that he would carry the bag.

The old man nevertheless tugged it off Justin's shoulder, smiling and saying in clear English, "Please, welcome to my home. I hear you are British. Would you like some tea? We have Five Roses, the best."

The young man, who had politely stayed behind Justin just outside the door, announced, "This man is Qxatta, he is the village's oldest man. A wise man."

Qxatta waved dismissively at the introduction.

Stepping into the hut behind Qxatta's bent frame and tapping stick, Justin passed into the shadow of the room — where he felt the temperature drop — and into a very different world.

The physical change Justin felt was the coolness created by a bare sand floor that had been dampened with water flicked by hand. A Kalahari breeze moved through the one window and out the door. The room's walls were the color of the soil.

Qxatta gestured that Justin should sit on what looked to be a child's wooden chair. As he motioned with one hand, he effortlessly folded himself onto the dirt floor. He kept his smile on Justin.

The small chair groaned under the American.

Am I going to break this? Me, small as I am?

Qxatta laughed and clapped his hands. "My Bushman furniture welcomes you, too. But maybe you are too big for it."

Justin pulled out his laptop, trying to adjust his weight to keep from breaking the chair, the only piece of furniture in the room.

"Thank you, sir, for meeting with me. This is my first time in a Bushman home. It is an honor."

"How can I help you?"

"I'm looking into some events that happened in the bush some sixty years ago. They happened south of here in Namibia and I was told the San people who had been in that area may have moved here. Some of them might know what happened."

The Bushman turned his head toward the one window. In a lowered voice, he said, "That was a bad time, sixty years ago, I was a young man. I don't know if I can help you. The bush is large, you know."

Justin shifted to move his legs out of the way of a young woman who entered the room, moving between them with tea and cups.

"Meet my great-granddaughter. She is one of many great-grandchildren I have. I've had two wives. Lots of children, grandchildren, and great-grandchildren."

The young woman turned with a perfectly white smile, "Pleasure."

Justin nodded his head, "Thank you."

She is even more beautiful than Sebastian's caregiver.

Recovering, he said, "Oh, my apologies," handing Qxatta the jars of honey, "These are for you and your family."

Again, Qxatta clapped his dark brown hands and smiled. "Honey. Of course. Perfect to help an old San with his memory. Do you know why, young Mr. British man, we love honey?"

"Sorry, sir. No. And I'm not British. I'm American and a lawyer."

"Well, America, that's a far drive, right?"

"Yes, sir, it would be. And there's the problem of the ocean."

"I know. Americans like airplanes. I worked forty years at the Grasslands Lodge. That is where I learned my English. I became a guide, doing game drives and teaching clients about Bushmen."

"It is remarkable how well you speak English."

"Thank you. Mr. American lawyer. Will you have some honey in your tea while I tell you why San people love honey? Every American tourist I meet loves this story when we are having sundowners." He looked at the open laptop and added, "Maybe you do not have time to hear it and want to get down to business like an American businessman. You tell me."

"Please, I would love to hear the story."

Qxatta's cheeks lifted with a full grin. "Honey is a gift for us, the San people, from the Creator. In the Kalahari there are some sweet roots and berries, but not as sweet as honey. The Creator knew this and gave us honey. But it is hard to find. Even Bushmen cannot track bees as they fly. The Creator knew this also. He gave us honeyguide birds so we could find the honey. Do you know about them?"

Justin sipped his tea. He shook his head, 'no.' His seat squeaked another 'welcome' as he did.

"These birds, they like to feed on the inside of bees' nests, but they cannot get in. The Creator told San people that we are to help this bird get into these nests and, if we do, the bird will be our honey guide.

"The birds come to us and ask us to follow. They guide us to a bees' nest. San people break the nest to get the honey. The bird eats and we eat.

"Do you like this story, Mr. American man? What is your name?"

"Justin. Yes, I like it."

"Now, Mr. Justin, if the San do not follow the honeyguide, if they do not give attention to the bird, it can get angry. The next time the bird finds you, it might guide you to a sleeping lion and not a bee nest."

His hands slapped together with a loud 'clap' as he laughed with white teeth flashing, "Then the honeyguide sees who eats!"

Justin smiled, lifting his cup in a toast, "Thank you. And now I will take some notes if that is all right."

Qxatta nodded.

"I understand your name, sir, is 'Kota.' Do you have a family name as well?"

"San names can be hard for you. It is 'Qxatta.' We have a 'k' sound we make in our language that is hard for Americans. Sort of a click. You can say it, 'Kota,' that is fine. That is my name, my only name."

"Thank you. As I told you, I am a lawyer. My client lives in New York. He has reported to us and others a violent event..." Justin felt the word clash with the peaceful surroundings of Qxatta's home. He would have to proceed delicately. "A most unfortunate event that happened west of Rietfontein about sixty years ago. We are trying to find someone who might have heard about it. I appreciate that the bush is a very large place."

Through a half-smile and squinting eyes, Qxatta said, "New York, I have seen on television. Very busy town.

"Have some tea. Perhaps I can help you. I heard many bush stories in my life. I have a large family. They also have ears. Tell me more."

Justin typed while he spoke.

"Two white hunters from South Africa were in the bush to protect white farmers from Bushmen. They ended up hunting Bushmen." Justin had done it again. His words were too raw, too brutal, in this place, before this man. He stopped typing to set gentle eyes on this kind old man. He continued more slowly, "One of the white men died. Have you heard anything about this?"

"Did you say these white men were hunting San people? One died?"

"Yes."

"There were many bad things that happened then. There were many problems between whites and San people. We moved here when I was a young man to stay away from problems."

"You don't remember hearing about these white hunters, one who died, and their hunt of Bushmen?" He had repeated all this too fast, with too much insistence, in the style of a New York lawyer. He could hear himself.

"We are now in a new place, white people, Bantu, and Bushmen," replied the old man, serenely, keeping close to his visitor but at a distance from the topic. "I am not sure it is good to look back. People must respect each other. It is that simple. That is what we do now."

Justin looked down at his tea and took a sip. Qxatta silently watched.

"Mr. Justin, you are asking a hard question, a question that takes my thoughts to a difficult time."

"Yes, sir. I understand that. But it might help some San people." Justin thought he had perhaps found a way in. "My client, who is asking these questions, would like to make a gift to the family of the Bushmen who were victims of this violence."

Qxatta stood easily from the floor by pulling his small body erect with his walking stick.

"Wait here. I might have something for your client."

Justin raised his brows as Qxatta shuffled behind him. *Where's this going?*

Qxatta stood in the doorway and spoke to one of his relatives. Over his shoulder, Justin heard him returning to the room, the speed of his shuffle consistent, slow, and the tapping of his stick, solid. Qxatta now held a bowl-like object.

"Here, my friend. This is a gift from us to your client. A serrated tortoiseshell to use as a bowl. We have used it for many meals. He will find it useful, too, when he cooks in New York."

Taking it carefully, Justin examined the shell and spoke softly, "Thank you."

This is gorgeous. The patches of brown on yellow shell are beautiful, framed all around by rolling edges. Inside is rough, dark. A coating likely left by years of family meals.

Can I take this with me or is this on an endangered species list and I'll be arrested?

Qxatta silently observed as the young man turned the shell over in his hands.

"Please tell your client that we are sorry he has questions about those difficult times. But answers about those days, those will not make him as happy as this gift. Take this instead. It will make him happier."

Rogue investigation leads to… a tortoise shell, thought Justin. He couldn't help shaking his head, ever so slightly.

The Bushman picked up the subtle sign.

"Now," he said gaily. "Can you eat something with us? It will be simple, but good San food. My wife is much younger than me. She is my second wife and is a wonderful cook. Sometimes she works in the kitchen at Grasslands."

"It would be my pleasure."

Qxatta called out in Bushman to the front of the house and got a quick response from several female voices.

"Good. All done. Now we wait a little." He squatted again." Tell me, young man, how many children do you have?"

"None. I'm not married."

"What? A man like you! I will tell none of the women here, otherwise you will not make it alone to your vehicle. My wife also will try to leave with you," he laughed.

Setting down the tortoise shell, Justin turned, raising his eyebrows at his host. "Kota," he ventured, "I still hope there is something you can help with. My client, who'll be very happy to receive your gift, has told several important people, including his own children, what happened in the bush and how that white hunter was killed." Here was a different tack. "No one believes him." He let that sink in, before adding, "He's old and they say he doesn't know what he's saying. If they believed what he says happened, it could be important for many people. And many San Bushmen."

Qxatta reached over for the tortoiseshell, picking it up. *I've insulted him.*

Smiling at his guest and turning toward the wall behind him, the elder San reached for a grey towel hanging from a nail. He wiped the shell cleaner, polishing the exterior, removing some soot.

Handing it back, he said, "There. That may be better for New York."

"Thank you. Very nice. I'll carry it carefully."

I won't get another chance. You, Kota, might be the key to Jon's vision, the foundation.

He pressed politely, "Do you know anything about what happened?"

Qxatta turned his head away from the young man. Justin could perceive a sigh, the man's small bare chest deflating. A long moment passed before he returned his gaze to the American, who could see, even in the half-light of the room, that his eyes were red, wet.

Wiping an eye he said, "Sorry, old man eyes. Yes, I heard about it. Your client is not lying, if he is talking about what I know.

"Young people in New York do not believe him because he is old. I understand. Even with San people, sometimes young people do not want to hear from their elders."

Justin set his iPhone on his satchel.

"Can I turn this on to record what you might tell me? *Damn. Again, too abrupt, too presumptuous.* Would that be all right?"

"Who will hear that recording? I am old and dying soon, but I do not want trouble."

"Only people in New York. No one here."

"If no one in Africa hears it, you can turn it on."

Part IV

Bush Guide

Chapter 16

Toushay

"To hear this story, you must know about my brother, Toushay. He was part of me, and me part of him. He was older, already walking when I was born. I cannot remember being without him when I was young. His mother, Nisa, was my mother's sister. She saw me born.

"When I was old enough to understand, I learned about the star that was in me. They taught me to find Toushay's star too. Our stars hunted together sometimes in the night sky."

Justin listened intently. "Sorry to interrupt, but you said the star was *in* you?"

"Yes. Maybe when we eat, I can explain.

"Toushay was taller than me, stronger and a better hunter. I learned from all the older boys, men, my father, my grandfather. But Toushay was my best teacher for many things.

"You know how we read spoor, follow tracks? You know that for us, the sand is a book? It tells us who was there, where they were going and when."

"Yes, I have heard."

"One day, Toushay and I were walking away from the family, together. He had his bow because he had already made his first kill. I had a strong stick. Like this one.

"We were following tracks of an aardvark. You do not see these animals in the day, they are so timid. We wanted to see where he was hiding and sleeping in the day so we could get him at night.

"You can easily follow them but finding them is hard. See, their back feet are big like this," pressing his palm on the sand floor.

"Their front feet are smaller, with sharp claws," digging three fingers into the floor. "You, see? Easy to follow."

Leaning forward to see the floor over his screen, Justin said, "I think so."

Can't see any difference.

"Maybe this aardvark takes us to a termite house that he found. We were two San boys, on the hunt for anything, even termites.

"As we followed the tracks, Toushay stopped at a strange print. It was square like this," drawing in the dirt a square made of four identical sides, about three inches on each side.

"In the middle, it was raised, like a small hill. I'll show you."

He picked up some sand and dropped it carefully in the center of the square to make a slight mound.

"He said to me, 'Qxatta, a monster lives here. Watch.' He took a small stick and put it under one side of the mound to lift it slowly. Under the mound was a silk door leading to a dark tunnel. He put the stick gently into the tunnel and pulled it out. Following it was a baboon spider, quite angry.

"He told me, 'Little brother, this baboon spider is dangerous. His poison is very strong. Always be careful if you see their holes or their homes covered like this one.'

"Young lawyer man, that gave me an idea for some fun.

"I waited a day or so. That way he forgot about the spider. Toushay was helping his mother scrape a steenbok hide. I was sitting in the shade close by.

"While he was busy, I made a perfect, just perfect, baboon spider nest. I was very careful. Then I called Toushay.

"'Brother, come here. There is another of those monster baboon spiders, I think. His house is right here. Close to us. It is dangerous.'

"Toushay looked closely at the spider home I had made. 'Back up, Qxatta. You are right, it is another one.'

"I pretended not to hear and said 'what, here?' I put my hand into the sand, up to my wrist, threw the sand at him and said, 'here?'"

Qxatta fell to his side laughing, "Ahh, Toushay jumped as high as he was tall, fell over in the sand and chased me with a stick until he caught me. We wrestled, throwing sand on each other, 'here is another spider for you,' we yelled."

"This was my brother, Toushay."

Justin had stopped typing back around 'monster spider' and just stared at Qxatta.

Misreading his response, Qxatta asked, "Does this bother you, Mr. American lawyer, this story of my life with Toushay? Are you patient with how we Africans tell stories?"

Justin smiled kindly. *I'm sure I'm onto something.* "Of course. I was just imagining that spider."

His host smiled patiently, "You need to know my Toushay to know about the white man that was killed. This is how we tell stories in the Kalahari. Slowly. Sometimes with spiders."

Qxatta shifted his small frame, chuckled, and prepared to continue.

"Toushay was at my side for my first kill, a young impala female. My father was behind us, but he let Toushay teach me. The wind had to be slight, toward us. Toushay moved me to where we knelt in the shade of a leadwood tree, watching impala graze near us. We checked the wind several times with dust we let fall from our hands.

"I did not hunt with a poison arrow until that day. They are so dangerous, you must hold them like this," mimicking an arrow in his hand, "placing them slowly on your bow, like this," putting the imaginary arrow on his walking stick that was now his bow.

"The bow I had was not big. It was small enough for me to hold and pull. We waited, together, my father behind us. Even now I can feel the heat of Toushay's body next to me. His head still, only his eyes moving, checking that I was ready and safe.

"I knew that he was to tell me when to pull and shoot. As the young female grazed closer to us, he inhaled, like this "whooo." I pulled back my arrow and waited. His knee touched my side, calming me. When it was the right time, he made a soft sound like this, 'click,' and I let the arrow go, hitting her in the side.

"The impala leaps and runs, the whole herd goes with her. We ran slowly after her, with me stopping to gather the arrow that had fallen out. We followed her easily until we found her.

"My first kill. Toushay was with me every step. That is how we lived."

"Is he still alive, Toushay? Does he live near here?"

"No. He is gone. That is part of the story you want to hear. Would you like me to tell you more?"

"Yes, please."

Qxatta adjusted his legs, pulling one under him. "Our family moved many times. You understand that about San people? We follow game and water. I was still a young man when my parents and other elders told us that white people wanted us to move away from where we hunted. We moved to a place that had little water. It was difficult.

"Some San people did not move. White farmers and soldiers took these people and made them work for them.

They were not paid. If they did not work, some were killed. We moved. It was safer. I told you; those were difficult days. Lots of problems.

"Some white farmers treated San well. Toushay and I were old enough to work, so we traveled together to a farmer who was good to San. We worked for him, watching his cattle, helping his plants. He and his family were kind, the pay was fair. We would work for several months and then return north to our family. It would take many days walking, maybe more than a week, to go home.

"Those days were good for us. Toushay and me, together. Sometimes we would find other San as we walked. Sometimes the military or white men would find us, and we had to show a letter from the farmer. Sometimes the letter did not work, and we had to work for another farmer without being paid before we could go home. San people were not allowed to live where we were traveling.

"Toushay and I listened for horses or trucks when we were in the bush. Usually, we could hear them and hide. We hid our bows. Bows and poisoned arrows were a big problem if white men found them.

"One afternoon, we were skinning a rabbit, talking with each other and not listening. Two German speakers came up to us, one on each side. They had rifles and told us we were in the Police Zone.

"My English was not good and I had no German. We showed the letter from our farmer. One man, he was very large with a beard, he looked at the letter and said it was not good. He threw it. They saw our bows and arrows, crushed them with their boots, saying we were 'criminals.' They told us to follow them.

"Toushay and I walked with them for an afternoon to their truck. There were other San in the truck. They were held together by a chain, so they did not run away. They put a chain on us, like the others, here, on our ankles. There was one San man who did not wear a chain. He worked for the Germans."

Qxatta moved his left leg forward so Justin could see the scars circling his slim ankle.

"The chains hurt us at night when we had to wear them so we would not run into the bush. During the day, at the beginning, we could work without them. The San who was not chained, the white men, and their dogs watched us."

Justin was enthralled. "Did you know these other San people in the truck? And the one who helped the Germans?"

"There were four men and a woman in the truck before we got to it. I knew some of the men. They were from another family we saw sometimes when we were hunting.

"The San man who was not chained, he did not look or speak to us. He did what the white men wanted. I did not know him.

"The white men drove us several days. It was very difficult. The open truck was hard and hot. The nights were cold. The metal on our ankles cut us. They gave us little water and bread.

"While we were in the truck, we spoke with the other San. They worked for a farmer and were taken in the bush by these men when they traveled to their home. One man seemed sick. He was old. Toushay put the old man's head on his leg to give him some comfort. At night, Toushay and the woman would sleep on either side of the old man to keep him warm. That is how Toushay was.

"We stopped at a place where a farm was planned. There was not much, only a small house of wood, some cattle held in a wire fence. And dogs. This German speaker had two large dogs.

"Am I telling you too much, Mr. Lawyer friend?"

"No, got it. This is good."

"We had to work for the tall German speaker, the one with the beard. He would laugh when his dogs frightened us. The work was hard, digging a new place for his home. We had little food. He chained us at night like he did on the truck.

"We were always cold at night. The German made us sleep in the same place on the ground with the chain on our legs going around a tree. We had no blankets. We had a small fire before we went to sleep but not during the night."

"What you're describing," Justin broke in, with a scowl, "we call 'press gangs,' when people are forced to work for no pay."

His mind shot to his undergraduate studies at Yale, his readings on Jim Crow — a chronicle of human suffering and abuse that paralleled Qxatta's account. The story of

Black Americans had not jumped from the end of slavery to the civil rights movement of the 1960s. In between was an entire century during which they had been subject to a whirlpool of abuse. Freed slaves left plantations, jobless, only to arrive in Southern towns that had anti-vagrancy laws. Unemployed, they fell into a system of arrests for loitering, followed by sentences that would be served working — for no compensation — for a white farmer.

Here, it's happening all over again, the same cruel exploitation, only in a different place with different means, different laws. The outcome's the same.

He told the old man indignantly, "Black Americans suffered the same thing in the South after slavery. But you hadn't been slaves! You were free people," he pleaded, not with Qxatta but with a now-absent persecutor. "Couldn't you complain to the military? You were in the Police Zone with permission, right?"

"The soldiers, they knew. Many farmers made San work for them for no money. One day some soldiers drove into the farm. They were young. I saw by how they looked at us that they did not like San. They drank beers with the German and his friend. They pointed at us with beers in their hands and laughed. Their faces said that they did not see us as men."

"Not as men? What are you saying?"

Qxatta stood. He dropped his walking stick. Taking both hands, he ran them slowly down his bare chest, down his legs and then over his face.

"You, see? I am a man. Those soldiers, they did not see me as you do. We are not humans to them. We are something else.

"Does a man listen to an animal complain that it is not being treated as a human? No. It is just an animal."

Justin held his gaze on this small man. Now so old, but standing with dignity, a dignity weighted by resignation. The contrast between who he was and how he had been treated reached deep into Justin. He breathed in the smell of the dirt floor — a sign of the poverty, the simplicity of this man and his home. A tear fell. He wiped his eye. Qxatta sat and rocked forward, laughing gently. "Ha. You, young man, you now have old man eyes."

"I suppose I do." Justin composed himself. "Do you want to tell me more?"

"The story is hard, young friend, but it goes where I think you want me to take you.

"The San who was sick, one morning, he stayed on the ground, when the German told us to start work. His family stayed on the ground with him. Toushay and I sat with them. No one stood to work.

"One San had some German. He talks to the German man. He says that we are not going to work, this man is sick, and we are leaving.

"The German was tall, taller than you. He lowers his head to the San man who was speaking German, like he was listening to a young child. He then walks away.

"He comes back with other German man who has a rifle and the dogs and rope. He shouts at us in German. Our

San friend says that the man tells us we must work. No one moves.

"The tall German unlocks the leg of the sick man. The other German has his rifle at us, the two dogs on their chains. The tall German pulls the sick man to a tree. He puts the rope around his neck and the rope over a branch. The other German goes, and they lift the old man by his neck off the ground. He is silent but his face turns blue. He tries to get his hands under the rope, but it is too tight. He wants to lift his arms to cover his face, so we do not see him die. His arms do not work anymore. His legs move and then stop."

Justin's sadness turned to horror and then — as he was his father's son — to determination. He would set this right, help Jon set it right. His coming here had been the right decision, it was going to pay off, to do good. *Imagine Rogers invoking ethics against me! Has no idea of ethics.* Pulling himself back to the moment, he crossed his arms and held his chest tightly, as if to keep himself in check.

"A man hanged, Kota. Murder. Didn't this enrage you? How are you not angry even now?"

Qxatta made a half-smile. "No anger today. Sorrow, but no anger. Let me help you understand.

"Do you know springbok?"

"What? No. Is that a place?"

"Ahh, my baby Bushman," he patted Justin's knee gently. "You need time in the bush with me. It is not a place. It is the most beautiful antelope in the desert. No animal more graceful.

"You know warthogs?"

"Yes."

"They are the opposite of springboks. They are ugly. They dig holes everywhere and eat plants we eat. They are ill-tempered and dangerous. They are not graceful.

"When I am in the desert and hear an animal, am I angry when I look and see it is a warthog and not a springbok? No. It is how the Creator made the world. There are warthogs and springboks.

"I am not angry today about the German warthogs."

"Are you saying you weren't angry then?"

"I was. Toushay was. We all are angry at these men. When they kill that man, it is bad. The tall German tells the San who spoke his language that we must work. We do not answer, but we get up.

"That day, and the other days, he puts chains on us during the day, one to another, so we cannot run."

Justin looked at Qxatta's face. The old man's eyes seemed heavier. He turned his gaze to the scars on Qxatta's thin, bare leg.

"This was slavery, what you have described. Slavery. How old do you think you were?"

"I am not sure of my age. Not married. Maybe sixteen or seventeen."

"That means this happened in the 1950s. Not very long ago."

"Yes, it was difficult then. German speakers, they are the most difficult. They are more difficult than English speakers and Afrikaners. German soldiers, you know, they kill many black people, Herero, Bantu people, in Namibia. Many, many people.

"This bad German, he let us go when we finish digging for him. He does not pay us. Only some bread and we left.

"We walk with the other San for a day into the bush to the North. I was too slow. I was sick. It is hard for me to walk after that German man's farm. The others leave Toushay and me. They are kind but want to find their families.

"Toushay helps me. I walk with my hand on his shoulder. My leg was bad from the chains, and I was weak. My leg is also bad from a sickness I had when I was young. See, it is smaller than the other leg, even now," he said pointing to his right leg with his stick.

"Would you like more tea? The food is coming soon."

"No, thank you. Please go on if you can."

"The leg makes walking difficult. After several days, I am too weak to walk. The afternoon is hot. Toushay put me in grass in the shade.

"He told me he saw some tracks of a 'nkoi,' porcupine in English. He knows 'nkoi' goes to bushes that have medicine. 'Nkoi' can take you to these bushes.

"This medicine bush has sharp green leaves with thorns. Sometimes they are hard to find. The 'nkoi' know where they are. You follow their track, seeing their quills dragging behind their little feet, showing you the way, find the bush they found for you, dig down with a stick and pull the root. Toushay brought a root to me, made a fire, and mashed the root. I chew it.

"I sleep after the medicine. He makes snares where he saw rabbit prints when following 'nkoi.' I wake to the smell of meat. I eat and am better. He was this for me. My brother.

"That trip was hard for us. When we find our family, we rest a long time.

"I remember they killed a kudu, a 'khrai,' and made beer. We were very happy."

"Sorry, Kota. You said they made beer from a kudu?"

"No, my American lawyer friend. Now you are no longer a Bushman," Qxatta laughed.

"You cannot make beer from kudu. You make beer from berries. You use skin from the neck of a kudu to make the place where the berry juice becomes beer. It is like a kudu bucket. Do you understand? Maybe you and I find a kudu and I can show you."

What's a kudu? Don't ask, keep him on his story.

"What happened to Toushay? You said he was gone."

"Now will you have more tea?"

Qxatta called out. His great-granddaughter arrived moments later with a steaming pot, her hair in new braids that caught the light, her arms strong, steady, smooth, a dark tan.

Justin looked up and then reverted his eyes a little too quickly.

I will get back here…

Qxatta picked up the attraction.

"I will tell her that you are not married. She finished school. She will prepare her bag to go with you and meet you at your vehicle. We can all go to New York for the wedding," he rubbed his hands against each other to signify the matter was settled, then chuckled into his tea.

"Kota, thank you. We'll see about that."

Keep the interview going, Jason told himself. *Get the missing pieces, get him to fit it all together.*

Glancing at his phone which was still recording, Justin searched for a transition. "I appreciate the importance of the Germans and Toushay, but I don't understand how they relate to the hunters from South Africa and the one that died."

Qxatta rocked back on his thin hips. His eyes smiled, "My American Bushman, what happened to you? You are like one of my great-grandchildren. You want to eat before cooking.

"Do you not know how to hunt? If I show you one single giraffe print, do you know if it is walking or running? Do you know if it is a bull or a cow? Do you know the direction it is going, or only the direction of the one print?

"You know nothing except that a giraffe is there. You need more to understand what you are seeing.

"It is that way with my story. That is why I tell you this long story, so you understand this giraffe we are tracking.

"Do you want me to continue?"

"Yes, please. I promise, I'm now reading the spoor."

He looked gravely at Justin, broke it with a grin and slapped his thigh. "Welcome back, my New York Bushman!

"Toushay and I go to the kind white farmer after the rains that year. We are careful as we walk there. We do not want German speakers to find us. If we make a fire, it is small. We pass several nights with no fire. That is dangerous. A lion maybe is hungry for young Bushmen.

"We work for that white farmer for several months. It is good work. Toushay and I become fat with his wife's food. She gives us meat every day and bread. We sleep under a roof. They have blankets for us.

"At the end of our time, this farmer gives us a letter to show to military or police. I put the letter in my quiver."

"You had your arrows and bow at the farmer's?"

"No. They are under sand with our spears, half a day from his farm. That way they are safe.

"Leaving that farmer and his wife, we are fat, I told you. But even fat men get hungry and thirsty. One morning I have a rabbit in my snare for dinner.

"As the sun set, Toushay points into the desert and says to me 'Brother, do you see that large fire? Maybe they have water, and we can share our rabbit for water. Maybe it is Germans. Or maybe English.'"

Qxatta looked fixedly at Justin. "It was South Africans, the two South Africans you want to know about."

Chapter 17

Human Hunt

"We are so quiet they do not hear us, but we hear them. They talk of hunting, one of them says, 'Buffalo are the most dangerous. One killed my partner.' The other one says, 'No, Bushmen are more dangerous than buffalo.'

"Toushay and I push each other by our shoulders. He whispers to me, 'How can a San man be more dangerous than a buffalo? Maybe if he is riding the buffalo.'

"We do not laugh with more than our eyes, but it is a good joke. We do not want these men to hear us. We watch them.

"Their voices are South African, not German. They talk about hunting. They are alone. No black people. Toushay says softly to me, 'They need guides and porters. They are here where there is no game. Maybe these men want us to help them, for money.' I say, 'Okay, but let's wait to see what they do today.' They are white men. We are careful. We watch."

Justin had caught his prey at last. "Were they militia? Were they *protecting* farmers?"

"Let me finish cooking this food for you.

"Those white men, they do not do much. We do not understand how they hunt in their camp. Maybe they are waiting for later afternoon and animals to come out.

"We leave them and go far so they do not see our fire. We cook the rabbit and eat. When the sun is down, we put sand on the fire and go to these white men to see if they are still doing nothing.

"We are silent and careful when we are close to them. San can be very quiet. The sun is gone. We watch them from dark brush near their camp.

"Toushay wanted to see them better, to get closer. We walk quietly to the edge of their firelight. They look like hunters. They have good rifles. They do not have much, only one pack each. No tent. They sleep on the ground under the sky like San people.

"'Let's talk with them.' Toushay whispered to me.

"I follow him a few steps and he stops. He holds his hand against me to keep me from moving.

"The larger white man is on his knees by the fire. The smaller man is on a log. The taller man hears us or feels we are there. He turns his face, to see us in the dark."

Qxatta turned grave and spoke solemnly.

"There is no animal that has this man's face. It is smiling but dangerous. His head is sharp like a snake. Black hair-like scales on his head. Looking where we are, he laughs and says something to his friend, and we see his teeth. They are not a man's teeth. They are small, sharp. Like a python.

"My American Bushman, this man is not normal. He is dangerous."

Justin nods silently, *Corroborates Jon's account, his description of Kuzman.*

Qxatta continued, "He cannot see us in the dark. But he knows something is there. He stands quickly, lifting his rifle, like this, fast, moving like a mamba, not a man," Qxatta says while flicking his wrist to put his hand up.

"Toushay is between the fire, the man, and me. He pushes me back with his hand, twice, telling me to go. I did not move. I go down on my knee to watch the man.

"This man moves from the light into the dark, knowing we are watching him.

"His rifle is not a farmer's rifle. It has a scope. The way he holds it when he is near the fire, I see he is a hunter. I do not see him when he goes into the dark outside the firelight, but I hear him put a round into the rifle. He does it slowly, but San people, we hear well in the bush.

"The smaller man also stands, but he stays where he is in the firelight and does not look dangerous. His face is normal, not angry like the large man."

Sounds like Jon, Justin thought. He hoped the old man was still alive. The story was coming together.

Qxatta pursued his narrative.

"Toushay pushes me on my head. He tells me with his hand to get up. I back up into the dark bush, as quietly as I can. We cannot see the tall man, but we hear him moving toward us. We hear his boots on leaves and grasses.

"Toushay says to me in a low voice, 'He is coming. Move quickly. There is something bad with him.'

"In my life, I never see Toushay frightened. My brother, Toushay, when he is young, he kills a lion that comes to hunt Bushmen close to our shelters one night. He is alone in the dark when he hits the animal with an arrow. Maybe the lion will attack and kill Toushay before the poison kills the lion. Toushay does not know, but his star is brilliant that night. The lion leaves our camp to die in the dark.

"This snake man, moving in the night to us, he frightens Toushay. That frightens me.

"San people live in the bush. We move quickly and quietly even in the dark. All the night we walk and run fast away from that man. We stop when we see the first morning stars.

"We are hungry and cold. We do not make a fire. We do not want to tell the ugly man where we are.

"With the sun, we keep moving north. We do not see the ugly man or the other white man when we look back over our tracks. With the evening coming, we think we are safe.

"We walk over an area of sand, no bush, no grasses. This is where many wildebeest come. They break plants with their horns and eat the grass down, so only sand is left. You do not want them in your house, these wildebeest."

Justin broke a smile. "Thank you, Kota. I'll keep that in mind."

"Good. They are not well-behaved. In this place that the wildebeest leave empty, you can see footprints we make, even with the many hooves that mark the sand.

"We stop after crossing that sand. Where we stop, several cattle are dead. Long ago. Many white bones and skulls are in the sand.

"My American Bushman do not think if you find water in the desert it is always good. Sometimes it is poison. I think that these cattle drank bad water and die but it is long ago.

"I leave Toushay at the place with the cattle bones. He is making a fire. He likes to do it by himself. He is strong and his hands do not get tired of spinning the fire stick. He has his way, every Bushman does. He always put pieces of dried mushroom in the hole where the fire starts. His fires are very quick.

"Do you know this about San people? Have you seen how to start a fire with cork branches?"

"No. I don't. Maybe I've seen it in movies."

"Let me show you after lunch and you can make a movie about me."

"Thank you, Kota. Before lunch, can we go back to the white men?"

"Yes, my Mr. Justin, my white Bushman, who is now like a San patiently tracking the giraffe in this story.

"Toushay is making a fire. I walk up a small hill. I remember it has large red rocks with big holes in them. The Creator threw them there. Many years ago, when he was angry with hyena. Hyenas do many bad things.

"Looking south, where we walked, with the setting sun on my right side, I see a light flash. It was for a second, then again. I watch where it was. I do not see the light again.

"What I see are two men, walking slowly in our direction. I do not see them well. They go in and out of trees and bushes. After some time, they cross an open area. I see that the man in front was bigger than the other man. This man is following our prints, he stops, pointing to the other man. I see it is the snake man.

"I run to Toushay and put sand on his small fire, to stop any smoke. We go fast from that place. We do not go far.

"Toushay says, 'Wait, those white men, they are going to stop at our fire. I know they will. We can be close to them, hiding in the bush, to see what they are going to do.'

"My brother and I go back to where we made our fire, the place with the cattle bones. We are silent and get very close behind them. They are foolish, looking only at where Toushay made a fire. They are not looking around the bush the way Bushmen do.

"We want to hear what they say.

"Laying down in sand close to them, this is what we see and hear."

Qxatta knew to weigh his words and be precise in drawing on his memory, without embellishment.

"The tall man kicks white bones and a skull that are close to our fire spot," he said in a measured manner. "He shouts in a big voice that we steal and kill those cattle. He says we are criminals.

"The smaller man says 'no.' The bones are very old, and our tracks are new. We are not killers of those cattle.

"They are angry with each other. The tall man is quick and points his rifle at the face of the smaller white man. He says the smaller man is wrong, we are criminals, and he is going to hunt and kill us. He says in an angry voice that if the small man does not help, he is alone in the bush. Maybe he dies like the cattle."

This happened the way Jon described. Rogers said pursuing this was unethical! Would've been unethical and tragic if I didn't. Coercion, duress. Valid defenses to a criminal charge of murder.

Locking his eyes on Qxatta, Justin asked, "Kota, what did the small man do?"

"The small man is angry, but we see he is afraid. The snake man can kill him, we see that. The smaller man's rifle stays down, he talks to the tall man. The mamba man just turns and follows our tracks. The small man's head is down, and he follows.

"American Bushman, I will teach you something. One man, alone, in the bush, even with a rifle, can die. I think the small man is afraid of dying if he leaves the tall man. Or the tall man kills him. The small man does not look like a man who can kill another man. He is like a child. He follows the snake man.

"This is how we know that these men hunt us. One wants to kill us; the other is behind him."

Justin interrupted, "Kota, this is important. Behind him, doing what?" The question elicited no response. "Behaving how?"

"He is behind him," repeated Qxatta. There was silence.

He knows what I'm trying to establish, thought Justin. He can't get me there, so he says nothing. Justin considered following Qxatta's lead. Leave it unsaid — *was Jon behind him protesting and interfering, or not? Don't say either. That leaves a doubt to exploit, a possible angle to defend Mr. Schmidt. Old Bushman's clever.*

But Justin had too clearly heard his client's words, too clearly understood his intent. What had to be established was not a defense, but the truth.

"Kota, the small man, behind the snake man, was he acquiescent?" It sounded coldly technical, out of Qxatta's English. Justin searched for another word. "Complacent? Was he passive?" He seemed to be getting closer.

Qxatta finished the job, "He was not stopping him, if that is what you are asking me."

The recording was running. Justin typed the words too, slowly, deliberately. *This is this evidence Jon needs!* He looked up so that Qxatta could continue.

"We leave that place quickly and go far into the bush away from those men.

"We only stop when the sky fills with stars. Toushay says to me, 'Little brother, if they are hunting us, we hunt them. We wait for them.'

"I say, 'No. We cannot hurt white men. Many San people die if we hurt them. Maybe the desert sends them home or kills them.'

"That night, Toushay listens to me. We do not wait for them in the bush to kill them. We stay hidden that night in brush, covered, with no fire. Like this," Qxatta rolled into a ball.

"The next day, we go quickly. We are very careful.

"Are you patient with this story, Mr. Justin? It takes time to find a giraffe, to know where it goes, so many years ago."

"Yes, I am. This trail is the one I have been looking for. Go on, please."

Qxatta adjusted his legs, using his stick to lift his body off the dirt floor, "There are many San people who travel where we travel. We find tracks of a group also going north. We know they are San prints because they have no boots. Bare feet. To fool the white men, we walk in their prints for a long time.

"Mr. Justin, this happens when you hunt. Maybe you put your arrow in an impala. It runs away from you fast, with the other impala, all mixing. How do you follow the one you have hit to find it when it dies if all the prints are the same? It is difficult. If you follow the wrong impala, you do not eat. Toushay and I know that, so we walk where other San people walk to make it difficult for the large man to find our tracks."

"You say that there were many other San people where you were. Did you see them, meet with them?"

"No. They pass that way several weeks before we do. The San group that went that way is not going to our home. After some hours, we leave their tracks and turn north to our home. Now, again, our prints are alone for the big man to find.

"We watch from a hill when the two white men follow our tracks that are mixed with the other San prints. The ugly man stops quickly where our prints leave the others and go in a different direction. He knows our prints. He is a hyena that is licking and smelling blood on grass. He knows how to find his game. He turns onto our tracks.

"There is a problem, you see, with my feet. One looks like other San feet. This one," pointing to his smaller right leg with the stick, "is different. It turns, you, see?"

Qxatta stood and walked a few paces.

"You see my foot, it is not like its brother. It tells you where I am. The ugly man, he can see that."

Justin shook his head. "Are you saying they were tracking you specifically, not just following in the direction you took?"

"Yes. I know this. They have other San prints to follow, and they leave those to follow us. We know they are hunting us.

"Toushay tells me, 'White men look for San people who steal or hurt cattle. I understand that. I do not understand white men hunting San for no reason, hunting people like animals. These are dangerous men. We can wait for them and kill them.'

"Again, I said, 'No. We can go more quickly. The large white man cannot go fast. They only have the water they are carrying. They cannot follow us very far.'

"We go north. They are following. We can see them."

Nisa, his great-granddaughter, came into the room with two apples and some warm, dark brown nuts on a light blue plastic plate.

"Thank you, my daughter," Qxatta said reaching for the plate.

"Here, my American friend, here are bush nuts. This story is sad and long. We need to smile again.

"These nuts, we call them, 'delicious' in San language," he laughs.

"Let me show you."

He held his walking stick close to its heavy end and used it as a hammer to hit a nut and then another. Shells broke, exposing warm, almost white interiors.

Justin juggled a few in his hand, they were so hot. Qxatta laughed watching him and said, "Perhaps we can have a fire some day in the bush, and I can show you how we cook these so quickly."

"They are sweet. Where do you find them?"

"There is a tree that gives them to us. I like them with green apples. Those grow in a store," he said, his eyes crinkling impishly.

"Thank you," Justin said, taking a bite of an apple, setting it on his satchel.

"Can you take me back to the story about these two men?"

Qxatta chewed a mouthful of nuts, eyes still compressed in a smile, but eyebrows reflecting seriousness.

"I tell this story many times. Toushay's parents have me tell them again and again as we sit at the fire. We sing about Toushay and what he does. We dance in a large circle around fires, women making music with drums and singing, and two San men with sticks like the white men's rifles following two others who dance in front of them. These two are Toushay and me, hiding from white men who hunt us. At the end of the dance, one turns to the white men, between them and the other dancer. He falls to his knees, hands on his face. Then he jumps up and dances the circle again.

"Toushay. A brave man."

Justin said, "I am not sure I understand. What happened? Is this when he died?"

"Yes. My brother and I stop at the end of that day with the white hunters coming for us. There is little light. We are far from the white men, too little light and too far for their rifles, we think.

"The white men see us. We see the small white man take up his rifle and point it at us. We see his scope catch some light when he does. We lower our heads, like this," feigning ducking.

"This smaller white man, he does not shoot. He puts his rifle down. We can see that the two white men are angry with each other. They wave their arms and rifles in the air. The small white man walks away, leaving the ugly man alone.

"I tell you how this man is dangerous and fast, like a snake. This big man, he points his rifle and shoots. Like that. No time. Just shoots. A mamba biting. Toushay moves in front of me when he does.

"Toushay and I fall on the ground. I am up before Toushay, who stays on the ground. I say, 'We go quickly now. This man is going to kill us.'

"Toushay stays down and does not speak. His face is in the sand. I see his blood under him, making the sand red. I turn him. The white man's bullet is here," putting a finger into the front of his hip.

"He looks at me with eyes that stop smiling.

"My Mr. Justin, this is how I do not have my Toushay. With the white man's bullet in him, he lifts on one arm, sitting. He makes no sound even with the wound that causes him great pain. His hands are wet with his blood.

"With red hands, he holds his bow like this and puts an arrow on his thumb," Qxatta feigned preparing an arrow to shoot.

"I know he is right. I do the same with my bow.

"We know where the large hunter is and send our arrows there, high into the sky and then down. We send two more and then two more. We hear his scream."

"I don't understand. You shot your arrows up to the sky to fall on him? Why didn't you shoot them at him?"

"He is far away. We sometimes hunt like that. We see some oryx together. Their horns up in the air as they eat or dig in the sand for melons. Their ears listening, their noses smelling and eyes looking for danger. We cannot get close because they run. We stay where we are and send our arrows to them like this," arching his right hand up and then down fast to the floor onto his fingertips.

"All we need is to hit one animal. The poison kills it."

"You hit the large white man?"

"We hear him from far away. The poison is strong. It's a bad death for a human or a snake. He screams for his friend, for his friend to kill him. His voice is the only sound that night. All the bush animals listen to him die. There are no animal calls, only his screams.

"I hold Toushay. It is cold with night. I pull grasses to put over him. He is larger than me, so it is hard for me to cover him with my arms. He does not speak or cry like the white man. He is San.

"He holds his hands over his face so I cannot see his pain. Shortly after, his star climbs into the sky, he is cold.

"When we die in the bush, it is not like white people dying. Our people who leave us, their time is over.

"I leave him there, his arms like this," crossing his arms on his chest.

"His blood is in the sand, on him. I know hyena are close. I can do nothing. I take his bow and quiver, cleaning dirt and blood off with my hands. I put them on his chest, under his hands, for his hunting with the stars. Then I leave him."

Qxatta breathed deeply and reached for his tea, his hand shaking.

"Kota. I'm so sorry. This must be difficult. We can take a break if you want."

"Thank you, Mr. Justin. Toushay and I hunt again soon. I am OK."

"If you want to keep telling me the story, tell me, if you know, what happened to the white hunters."

"I know what happens because I see it.

"The snake man who kills Toushay, I hear him in the night. He is loud and then silent. He is dead.

"The other one is alive. He hunted us with the tall man. Together. The small man, he could have stopped the tall man, or he could have left. He did not.

"When Toushay wants to kill both men, I say 'no.'

"Now I go to hunt the small white man, to kill him."

Chapter 18

Prey and Predator

"I think he is near his friend, the tall hunter, who dies in the night. Before the sun, I leave Toushay and go behind the white men. It is not hard to find them. The smaller hunter makes a lot of noise. He talks to himself and moves brush and branches over the dead white man.

"I watch him for several minutes. My bow is in my hands. I can shoot him no problem. The rifles and packs are close to a tree away from him.

"We are deep in the bush. There is one dead white man already. That is a problem. Maybe they do not find this one white man before hyenas find him. When white men find a dead white man in the bush, many times they are angry and hurt San or Bantu people.

"Two dead white men is a big problem. I choose to let the desert kill this other white man. Maybe no African people are hurt if the desert kills him.

"I take everything. His food. His water. His rifles. He tries to follow for a little, yells at me and then is quiet.

"This white man alone in the Kalahari dies with no water and food. Or a lion gets a full belly. His bones go like those cattle bones, white in the sun.

"I hide the rifles and packs under sand. I do not take them for me. I am not a thief.

"I leave him with nothing and walk north to my family.

"The day is hot. I am sad. I am alone. I know the white man is dying but I do not have my Toushay.

"I find some roots that are sweet. They help me.

"That night I watch the stars to see if Toushay's star is hunting. I do not see it.

"When I do not see his star, I am more angry at the two white men. One, I know, is still walking, maybe dying, but walking. When the sun comes up, I listen to Toushay. I go hunt to kill this man. My anger is that much.

"Finding him is easy. I go where he leaves his dead friend. The dead face is up. I look at the man who kills my Toushay. It is swollen, large, fat, a dead snake. I move branches and dirt off his body to make hyena's kitchen.

"I see the pain in his face. His skin where the arrow hits is dark and open. Already there are hyena prints around the body and flies. 'Good,' I think. 'Come eat him.'

"I go hunt the other man. Tracking a man in boots in the Kalahari is simple. The smaller man's prints are clear. First, I see he walks straight south. He follows backward the tracks they make when they hunt us.

"By afternoon, it is very hot. I have no water. But I am San. I can live like that. A white man, with no water, he has problems.

"By late that day, the boot tracks they make when they come to hunt us are hard to see. Tracks are lost among many rocks. At least for a white man they are lost. A San can find them.

"This white man, he has no water or food. He does not know his way. The trail is now lost to him. It is hot. Kalahari hot.

"Mr. Justin, if you are an impala or oryx and you do not want to die when you come to bushes or trees, do you walk into dark shadows made by the afternoon sun, or do you walk on the side that is still in the sun?"

"Not sure. Maybe I go on the side where the sun is."

"Good. Maybe, Mr. Justin, you are still my white Bushman! You know this.

"Oryx and impala do not walk into dark shadows because they cannot see the lion or leopard who is waiting. The low sun makes the bush dark to hide the predator. You want to go to the side with the sun, so you can see who is in front of you.

"This white man, he is no different than those animals. He knows he comes from the south, so he walks that way. But when he comes to trees or bushes where shadows make the left side dark, he goes on the right, to the west, to have the sun help him see what is in front. This way he walks away from his trail. The Kalahari kills men like this.

"When the sun is down, I stop hunting this man. I know he does not walk at night. Too dangerous to walk in the dark where only lions and leopards see well. He finds a tree maybe.

"I see him early the next day. Stupid, this hunter of people. Now he is walking to the east around trees and bushes. This way, he is not on his old tracks. He is more lost."

Justin blinked, furrowed his brow.

"You look at me like one of my great-grandchildren. You do not understand how he can lose his own trail. Come with me."

Qxatta stood abruptly and, without saying more, left the hut, his stick rhythmically accompanying the soft padding of his bare feet. Justin watched him leaving the room.

I don't know what he's up to but I'm game.

Justin placed his laptop on the small chair and followed, squinting as he stepped into the bright sunlight. A few boys ran over to them. Qxatta hardly looked in their direction and waved them back. The elder Bushman stopped and fixed on a tree outside of the settlement.

Pointing with his stick, "That is the direction we are going. Imagine there is a trail, your trail, that goes from here to that tree. Remember it but keep your head looking at the ground."

He walks off without glancing at Justin. They arrive at a thick thorn bush that has branches reaching almost to the ground. Qxatta uses his walking stick to point, as he instructs Justin.

"Now, my American Bushman, imagine this side, the right of the bush, is dark, because the sun setting on the left side, over here." He waved his stick toward either side of the bush. "Do you walk into the shadow on the right side where you might not see a lion hiding or do you go around it to the left so you can see if a lion is there?"

"I would go around it to the left, on the sunny side."

"Good. You are not dead yet. Follow me."

Qxatta walked around the bush to the left, with Justin closely following him and glancing over his shoulders right and left. *Are there lions here?*

They approached a cluster of small trees.

"American Bushman who is not yet dead, if these trees are dark on the right side and there is light on the left side, which way do you go?"

"To the left again."

Qxatta tapped Justin's thigh with his stick, "I am happy you are not dead still. Follow me."

The odd pair of an aged Bushman and a young American lawyer continued the process for half a dozen more trees and bushes. Each time, before they went further, Justin had to say out loud that he would go left around the obstacle to stay in the light.

Stopping after they rounded a final group of bushes, Qxatta tapped the ground with his stick, "Now, look up, where is the trail we were following? Where is the tree that was our destination and where are we?"

Justin scanned around. The collection of huts, the settlement, was behind him, well off to his right. The boys who had been waved away stood looking at them from atop a termite mound. The tree that had been their destination was still in front of them, but also off to their right, not straight in front of them as it had been at the beginning. They had wandered well away from the imaginary 'trail' that ran directly from the village and the tree.

Both hands on his stick, Qxatta said, "You understand how this white man lost his trail?" Not waiting for an answer, he turned toward home, "Now, let's go back to my house, so I can help you find yours."

Justin's rickety chair creaked a welcome as he sat again in the hut. Qxatta had a satisfied expression when he lowered himself onto the dirt floor and got back to his story of tracking the remaining white man.

He raised his hands, "I see the weak steps of this lost hunter of people. He walks like this, like he is a drunk man," curling his fingers and palms in a wave pattern.

"I see where he is going. I go there to wait.

"I am down like this in the shade of a cork wood tree," Qxatta said getting up on his feet, sitting back on his heels, walking stick now again his bow.

"I have my bow ready to kill this man."

Sitting back down, he laughed, "You know, I do not. I do not kill this man. My anger is leaving me. By the time I see him, I am only sad."

Justin smiled at him, "Yeah, I think I know."

"This white man walks toward me. He does not lift his feet. His boots do not leave the sand. They are too heavy for his legs. He comes close. I stand with my bow ready. My arrow points at him. This man, he is so tired. When I stand, he stops, looks at me, his arms hang down, over like an old man. His eyes are almost closed.

"He raises a hand over his eyes to see me better, to see me and talk to me, 'Go ahead. You and your friend kill me.'

"When he said that, I hear his voice. It is not a killer's voice. It is the voice of a young man, a high voice, a voice of a broken man. He does not know Toushay is dead.

"I hold my arrow, its poison ready to kill him. I point it at him for many breaths. His voice troubles me. He is not an evil man. I put down my bow and hold my arrow in my fingers.

"The man lowers his hand and sits in the sand. This white man puts his head down, like this," Qxatta says bending his head into his chest.

"He looks into the ground. He is a sick wildebeest ready for lions to take him.

"I do not need to kill him.

"I turn and leave. I walk to the North until night. I make a fire. When the first stars come out, I look again, searching for Toushay's star. When the sky is filled and half the night is gone, I see it. It is coming across the sky, hunting other stars. I smile to myself that my brother is hunting again. I sleep well. I dream of him.

"I am hungry that morning. I find a brandy bush with berries. When I eat, I think of that white man's weak voice and his hunger. I took his food, and he is hungry.

"People must respect each other. This is why there are problems between whites, San and Bantu. We forget to respect each other as human people.

"I go back to him. He is not moving on the sand. Maybe he is dead. I stand away from him and say, 'Hey, white man.' He lifts his head. He is not dead.

"I put berries by his head. He reaches for them, his hand shakes and he eats. I give him more.

"His arms are weak when he sits up. His face tells me he is dying. He says, 'Thank you.'

"I do not say anything. I look at him when he eats berries, I give him. This mans who hunts people, my Toushay. I give him food, not my words. I do not accept his 'thank you.'"

Justin cut in, "Kota, I have some pictures of our client when he was a young man. Would you tell me if this was the man?"

Justin turned his screen toward Qxatta. Its pale blue light filled the back of the small home, Qxatta casting a thin shadow against the wall. Justin glanced over Qxatta's shoulder.

There is nothing in here. Nothing but dirt walls, some sacks and bedding.

Flipping through images, Justin said to Qxatta, "This is our client when he was young and hunting in South Africa. This is him with his father.

"Is this the man?"

It took Qxatta no time. "That is him. His eyes I know. His face, I see still in my mind."

Justin sat back. *It's done. Mr. Schmidt was right all along. It happened.*

"Kota, the man in these photos is Jon Schmidt from Cape Town. Are you certain this is the man you are describing? It has been sixty years. You might be wrong."

"Mr. Justin, you know San people live out there, in the bush, in the desert," gesturing out the door.

"There, you live if you see, if you hear. We see our world. We know plants by one leaf. We read tracks better than anyone. Every detail is important, so we see everything. When I look at his face years ago, I see it. I do not forget that man."

"Kota, I have told you that people do not believe Mr. Schmidt. How certain are you that this man was part of the hunt of you and Toushay?"

"Mr. Justin, in my life, no man treats me like these men. Yes, some white men make me work without money or much food. But this man and his snake friend, they track us like animals, not people. When I see him, when I see his face when I give him food, I see him. I see him the way we see other things in the bush. I remember. This is the man.

"You ask me, am I sure? You see the two stones in the sand when you come to my house, the stones with painting on them?"

"Yes. I wondered what they were."

"That is where two of my children are. I am as sure of that as I am sure of this being the man."

Justin's voice softened apologetically, "I hope I didn't offend you. I had to ask. I'm sorry about your children."

"It is a long time now.

"It is OK. I know you have important questions."

Turning the computer back around, Justin said, "Thank you. To summarize, you recognize the man in these pictures, and he is the man who hunted you. You have no doubt."

"Yes."

Justin's hands tremble. *What have I forgotten? Need to firm this up.*

"After you gave him food, did you leave him?"

"No. He eats and smiles at me. He speaks with that small, weak voice, saying, 'Thank you' again.

"I do not speak to him, but watch. He stands. His hands down. His boots, too heavy for him, stuck in the sand.

"I walk away from him, toward the tracks we made days before. I will take him out of the desert. He stands still.

"I wave my hand like this," gesturing 'come here.'

"He does not move. I do it again. He steps toward me. He begins to follow me.

"He is slow, this dying white man. Many times, I wait for him after a few steps.

"It is like that. I have no food for him. He is slow when he walks. Sometimes he sits. I wait for him.

"With the day almost gone, when he sits, he watches me make a fire. His face looks at me with eyes of a young man who dies. Sad. Not like an old man who dies. I am sad for him but do not talk to him.

"I take branches and put them close to the fire for him. I walk from it and tell him with my hands for him to go to the fire. He does.

"He has his whole body on the sand, around the fire. He does not look up. I see him blow on the fire and add a branch.

"I leave him but do not go far.

"Other San travel where we are. Justin, you remember I tell you this?"

"Yes."

"When San travel, we can put water in the sand. We take an ostrich egg, you know them?"

"Yes."

"They are large and can hold water. We have water in them and put the shell with water under sand. We mark the place in a way that San can see. I find one of these places."

"Wait, how does this work? Doesn't the water leak out or sand get in?"

"There is a hole we make, big like a finger. We put grasses to keep the water from leaving or sand from getting in. It keeps water for a long time. Many San live in waterless areas because of this way of hiding water. I have one I can show you."

Qxatta calls out of the room. His great-granddaughter replies with a voice that Justin found as beautiful as her presence, "Yes, Grandfather." She enters the room with an ostrich eggshell, yellowed and brown with use and age. Qxatta takes it with both hands. It is almost as large as his head. He hands it to Justin.

"Here, you can feel it. Do you want me to fill it with water for you?"

"No. Not necessary." Justin weighed the eggshell with his hands and gave it back. "What did you do when you found the water?"

"I drink some and go to your Mr. Smith."

"Schmidt."

"Yes, the white man. He is laying down near the fire. He hears me when I say, 'Here is water.'

"That is all I say.

"He sits up with two hands reaching. I put the egg in his hands, I hold it for him, he is so weak. Our hands touch. He drinks, I see his face very close. His eyes. They thank me, the way a young child thanks you with his eyes when eating.

"This is why I know the man in your pictures is this man.

"I let him drink water. I leave him and walk back into the bush. He is better now. He has fire and water in his belly.

"When the sun rises up, I find him again. The fire is out, just smoke. He sleeps around it.

"I say, 'Follow me.' He is a baby impala when he stands, weak, shakes with first steps, and then is OK.

"That day, he is very slow. By early afternoon, he falls and does not get up. I have no more water for him but make a fire. I leave him like that.

"Around us, I see tracks of a kori bustard. You know these birds? Big like this," holding his hand a meter off the floor.

"I find her nest and leave a snare. I go back to the man several times to keep the fire alive.

"That night, I sleep in the bush close to him so I can see his fire. Many times, I leave my fire to put wood on his.

"With the morning stars, I find a kori in my snare. While he sleeps, I cook the bird. A bat-eared fox smells the meat and comes to look at me. I tell him, 'Not yet. The 'Mzungu' must eat. Come back for bones we leave for you.'

"If you want to ask this bat-eared fox some questions about this food for the white man, maybe I can find him for you," Qxatta says flashing his eyes at Justin.

Justin looks up with a silent grin while typing.

"Maybe you can give me his name and address later for my report."

"Of course! He remains a friend of mine."

Qxatta settles back with his stick straight up, clearly satisfied with his bush humor. He taps his stick, back to work.

"I wake this white man with the smell of bird meat. He eats and is sick. But he eats most of it. He thanks me many times.

"He stands with more strength and follows me that afternoon. I make another fire for him. I do not catch any food that night. But he is doing better.

"After these days, we find the trail he and his friend use to come hunt us. There are vehicle tracks. We follow them to the edge of a white man's farm.

"I wave to him to go. He stops and looks at me. His eyes are not dying now.

"Many white men cry. They cry at strange times. I see them cry when they see an elephant for the first time or a leopard. This man does that. He cries. He looks at me with his face wet like a child.

"He puts his hand out. I do not take it. He is a man who hunts human people, my Toushay. I walk away. I go home to my family."

Part V

Night Sky Alignment

Chapter 19

Legacy Stain

Justin fidgeted with the binder Julia handed him. It was identical to the one lying open on her desk. Both were labeled, *"Attorney Work-Product; Privileged and Confidential; Schmidt Review."*

Rogers entered with an antiseptic, "Good morning," addressed to no one. Justin did not acknowledge him. He, too, carried a binder.

Julia's office reflected her efficient discipline. Her glass-top desk was clear of papers. To her left were a monitor and keyboard. There was nothing else. Behind her was her wall of honor that displayed photos of her with notable clients and politicians. Among them was a photo of a leopard, a close-up of the animal's face framed by green leaves. Jon had given it to her years ago.

Justin opened the binder. In it were a summary of findings, transcripts of his interviews, supporting photographs and articles, and a memory stick attached to the back cover. All the evidence was on the stick.

"Justin, you may have heard that Jon is still unresponsive. He's alive, but for how long, is anyone's guess? Not long though."

She turned to the binder.

"We took the information you relayed before your return flight and prepared this for our meeting with Paul. It's in an hour." Her tone was characteristically professional, in the style of the label on the binder. She let slip, "Your work, your initiative... I was moved by reading about Jon's experiences as recounted by this Bushman. Your photos of the man and his family brought it home."

Rogers grunted. "Unusual, to say the least. Comprehensive."

She ignored him. "We sent the binder to the other side, ahead of our meeting. I'm confident we can nail this shut for Jon."

An hour later, Julia was intentionally, dramatically late for the meeting. Facing her on the other side of the conference table, with a copy of the binder in front of each, were Paul and Jon's two sons. Only Richard, the youngest, greeted her.

"Richard, Gareth, thank you for coming. I know this is a hard time for you with your father's condition. How is he?"

Paul responded for his clients, "He's not regained consciousness, as you know."

Richard added, "He's doing all right. Thank you. And thank you and your firm for the fresh flowers every day."

Julia shifted her gaze to Gareth. "Our pleasure. You have the materials. You may have questions. Justin, give them your affidavit."

As copies were distributed, Julia explained, "This affidavit, to which Justin swore under penalty of perjury, gives you step-by-step how he investigated Jon's story, as well as confirming that the recordings, transcripts and photos in your binders accurately reflect what he found."

Flipping slowly through the document, Paul did not look up. It was five pages, single-spaced. "Justin, you understand there'll be serious civil and criminal consequences for your firm and for you personally if… "

Julia had coached Justin. He looked squarely at Paul and recited, as if reading from a card, "I fully understand the implications of my affidavit. It and the materials it references are accurate. I am aware of its legal import."

Paul proceeded to his next tactic.

"Justin, as you know, your firm is aiming to set up a foundation that it will administer, and for which it will receive substantial fees." If Justin wasn't a liar, maybe he was corrupt — so went this line of argument. "In this context," Paul continued, swelling and smirking, "don't you think it's a *convenient coincidence* that, of all the Bushmen in Africa, you find the one, the only one, who knows anything about all this?"

Gareth and Richard moved to chime in. Julia raised a finger, elegantly. The men waited.

"Justin's affidavit speaks for itself, as do the recordings and photos." Her voice lowered, smoothing out. "Unlike you, we had no preset conclusion. We conducted a legitimate inquiry. Our methodology was sound. We went where the facts took us."

Her tempo increased. "It was no *convenient coincidence* that Justin met with border guards where Mr. Schmidt said he crossed into South Africa after the hunt. Anyone would have started there.

"They didn't know about the incident — we told you about this dead end. They referred Justin to a retired colleague, who confirmed some facts but was convinced Jon murdered his hunting partner. The farmer's widow had the same assessment. We have been completely transparent with you about this preliminary information that undercut Jon's account. On receipt of this information, we, ourselves, instructed Justin to terminate his mission and return home. That's in the affidavit."

"Julia, please," huffed Paul sarcastically. "Oliver North here just did what was right, without his boss knowing?"

She looked Paul over, then looked over Justin, as if comparing them. "A competent lawyer listens to his client, keeps an open mind. Gets out in the field. Sees what those sitting in skyscrapers can't. First-hand observation — the kind of thing that forms a sound basis for judgment. Then acts on that judgment."

The speech had been tight, closed. Paul saw there was nothing to pursue here. Better to try to discredit items of evidence. With fingers splayed he plucked visibly at the little flags he had placed down the right side of his binder, on various pages, intending that each would sound a note of doubt.

Julia cut him off. "It was no convenient coincidence," she said, continuing her rebuttal, "that in Rietfontein, people knew where the Bushmen had gone. That is as unremarkable as people in Santa Fe knowing where the Navajo went.

"It was no convenient coincidence to have found Kota in a place where many San people moved to escape persecution. He was in the most likely place he could have been.

"It's no coincidence that these people — and hardly convenient for them — suffered inhumane treatment. It's a matter of historical record. Their treatment was criminal and unjust by design. The most extreme form of this injustice — also documented, and regrettably not uncommon — was what we have encountered here: a hunt. A recreational hunt of human beings."

There was silence. No one even rustled a page.

"Justin located Kota, a victim of Jon's tragic decision to join in the hunt. He didn't interrogate him. You've heard the tapes. He listened patiently, respectfully. Kota was reluctant to talk at all about what happened. But he did, and what he told us is credible and persuasive. It explains Jon's persistence, his desire to make this right.

"In fact, I can tell you that Jon put it to us more starkly," she told his sons directly. "He said his sin was so grave that he had 'killed the moon.' He has directed us to rebuild it.

"That, Paul, I do not see as a coincidence or convenient. That, I see as our common obligation to this man and these Bushmen."

Julia fixed on Paul briefly, then raised eyebrows at Gareth, her eyes sweeping in Richard.

Paul tried to recover the advantage. "You haven't answered my question," he shot back, leaning forward in an attempt to dominate her. "My clients demand to know…"

But Gareth stood, pushing his chair loudly away from the table. His binder was open to a full-page photo of Qxatta standing with his wife and great-granddaughter in front of their dwelling. He slid it across the polished wood table toward Julia.

"I'm done, Paul. This story is bad, in fact, worse than we feared. After everything, this man should've let dad die or killed him. But this man, this Bushman, I have no idea why, he forgave him, went back, and *saved* our father. For Chrissake!"

By now Richard was also standing, but limply. In a voice that was fatigued, empty, he added, "I'm also done. Thought I knew my father. I listened to Kota's interview. I want nothing to do with any of this."

"If this gets out," Gareth still standing said dismissively to Paul, "how do we explain that dad was a racist coward?

"Give them what they want, what dad wants. Just get a watertight non-disclosure. I want these files, recordings, photos, everything — destroyed. We bury this. It never happened."

Gareth's perennially tanned face had gone deeper dark from humiliation and anger. He addressed Justin as he headed to the door, "We get it. We aren't monsters. You neglected to put that in your report."

He stopped at the doorway and turned to Julia. He gestured toward Justin — not a finger point, but a flat palm. "A final condition, Julia. This young man, he heads the foundation effort. It's what dad would want. It's what Richard and I want."

On hearing this, Justin thought of the simplicity — and the power — of what he had found in Botswana: the water in the ostrich shell, the berries, a small black man sitting on his dirt floor wearing little more than a smile.

He thought of his client. *I managed my first hunt. I found your trail. I followed it where you said it would lead.*

And he thought of his father, dead at his desk beneath Dr. King's photo with its legend, "Courage Knows No Color."

Chapter 20

New Moon

"Mr. Schmidt, sir, can you hear me?" Patrick brushed back the remaining white strands from a face that was immobile, save for sightless eyes that rolled under half-closed lids, and lips that formed unspoken words.

"Mr. Schmidt, is that a person? What's a Cooseman?"

Jon was unresponsive but for faint mumbling. Behind closed eyes that jerked in seeming panic, he was again in the Kalahari of his youth. He thrashed without moving, wrestling with haunting regret in a place only the dying can go.

"Hold still," Jon told Kuzman as he struggled to hold the larger man against the dirt. "Let me see the wound."

It's no use. His shoulder is already dark. Poison is going through him. I should leave him. He's dead anyway. Staying is suicide.

"Stop screaming!" Jon whispered desperately at him. "They're close. We'll have no chance with your screaming."

Kuzman could not hear, his head spastically falling side to side in near delirium, left hand clawing at his right shoulder. "Kill me, please!"

"I'm not going to kill you. Stop yelling."

Bloody fitting end if you ask me.

Hours passed until Jon could at last turn his face to the new night sky, his hand still resting on the chest of the Yugoslav. His ears strained to hear what had been their prey, now their hunters — a footfall, a crack.

Nothing. Where are they? Hours since you stopped screaming. Can't feel breathing.

What? ID card in your shirt pocket? I'll take it if you don't mind. You'll not need it, and a jackal could choke on it. Likely an inquiry about this. Might help if I have it.

"Here, Kuzman, I'll do you the courtesy of folding your arms, as if you're finally in church."

Can cover you, too. Can't just leave your body open for all takers.

After a cold night with no fire, back against a tree, rifle in hand, and his fear magnified by Kuzman's corpse close by, Jon stood and stiffly surveilled the bush. He assembled their gear and rifles at the base of a nearby tree and returned to Kuzman for a last time.

Kneeling near the body, mounded with sand, acacia and leadwood branches, Jon became chilled and anxious to move. He pushed a bit more sand onto Kuzman. "This is it. Best I could do. I should've shot you when I had the chance. Just couldn't do it.

"I'll let the authorities know you died out here."

A noise behind made him spin around — footsteps, breathing, rifles clacking together.

Minutes later, well into the scrub, away from Kuzman's corpse, Jon gave up, hands on both knees, panting.

Bushmen thieves. I'll never catch them. Took both rifles and packs!

He yelled into the thicket now surrounding him, "Come back! It was him, not me. I didn't shoot. For the love of God, give me at least my pack, some water!"

Hours later, afternoon shadows traced after Jon, as he walked among ever-darkening bushes. Before the light failed, he had already lost the tracks he had been following.

Up into this tree, branches are low enough. Safe maybe. Wait for tomorrow. Maybe a leopard'll find me. Would be a right smart end to this.

In the morning, descending from the tree with the warmth of the sun on his back, Jon resumed his search for tracks that would take him back to the farm, to his truck. Steps unsteady, fear, thirst, hunger. No weapon, alone, he was now a dagga boy. He would survive only if he could sense danger and respond before an attack.

He failed.

The short, skinny Bushman — a mere teen — said nothing. He held his arrow steady, only meters away. Its dark poisoned tip was aimed at Jon's chest.

A boy. We hunted children. God save me!

Head turning right and left, he said, "Where's the other guy?"

The Bushman did not respond or move. Jon's voice was weak with thirst and choked with his coming death.

"Go ahead. Kill me. I deserve it."

The young Bushman relaxed his bow. Arrow pointed down, he studied Jon… for decades.

The Bushman stepped toward the white man. He was stiffer, bent, old. His bow was gone, a walking stick now in his left hand. His right extended, trembling slightly. His face opened with a smile that broadened as he approached, deepening creases around his eyes.

He took Jon's thin grey hand, "I sent you a gift with that young lawyer."

Meeting Qxatta's eyes, Jon said, "I know. Thank you. I left one for your family."

The two men walked side by side into dark brush. Neither left prints in the soft sand.

The End